WHAT READERS ARE ~~SAYING~~

"Travis Thrasher's stories f
be invested in and rooted
story that leaves you wan

TOM FARR

"If you like compelling characters with an intriguing premise,
a bit of music, danger, and high school angst thrown in for
good measure, all wrapped up in a story that explores themes
of God's redemption—get ready."

JOEL DAVIS

WITHDRAWN

"Thrasher excels in making you feel what his characters are
going through, whether or not you can personally relate.
Only the best fiction can do that, and Thrasher does it so
easily you barely notice until you start feeling along with the
character. Thrasher is a writer unlike any other. He's written
love stories, adventure, mystery, horror, Christian movie
novelizations, and even a few extrapolations of country
music songs. And he's good at them all. But creepy-YA-life-
is-beyond-weird-coming-of-age stories? That's definitely
what he's best at."

JOSH OLDS, LIFEISSTORY.COM

"Prepare to fall in love with a character who doesn't realize his own strength but keeps standing and fighting for the underdog anyway."
MELINDA BAUR

"An amazing and uplifting feat of storytelling with real, believable characters you can't help caring about. This book—the entire series—is a must-read, not only for young adults, but for anyone who enjoys great writing."
DON BEARD

"The characters in this book have remarkable resilience. That's a trait that keeps readers interested in the story. There's so much heartbreak swirling around Brandon and Marvel, yet they are being pulled forward toward the plan God intended for them. Each time I read a portion, I was left thinking about the two of them. That is a sign of a good book."
JENNIFER CARTER

THE BOOKS of MARVELLA

A NavPress resource published in alliance
with Tyndale House Publishers, Inc.

NAVPRESS⦿®

NavPress is the publishing ministry of The Navigators, an international Christian organization and leader in personal spiritual development. NavPress is committed to helping people grow spiritually and enjoy lives of meaning and hope through personal and group resources that are biblically rooted, culturally relevant, and highly practical.

For more information, visit www.NavPress.com.

ISBN 978-1-61291-624-8

Cover design by Studio Gearbox

Cover illustration by David Carlson/Gearbox. Copyright © by NavPress. All rights reserved.

Interior design by Dean H. Renninger

Published in association with Folio Literary Management, LLC, 630 Ninth Avenue, Suite 1101, New York, NY 10036.

Scripture quotations are taken from the *Holy Bible*, New Living Translation, copyright © 1996, 2004, 2007, 2013 by Tyndale House Foundation. Used by permission of Tyndale House Publishers, Inc., Carol Stream, IL 60188. All rights reserved.

Some of the anecdotal illustrations in this book are true to life and are included with the permission of the persons involved. All other illustrations are composites of real situations, and any resemblance to people living or dead is coincidental.

Library of Congress Cataloging-in-Publication Data

Thrasher, Travis, date.
  Wonder / Travis Thrasher.
    pages cm. — (The books of Marvella ; [2])
  ISBN 978-1-61291-624-8
  [1. Murder—Fiction.   2. Bullying—Fiction.   3. Love—Fiction.   4. Christian life—Fiction.]   I. Title.
  PZ7.T411Wo 2015
  [Fic]—dc23   2014023630

Printed in the United States of America

20   19   18   17   16   15   14
 7   6   5   4   3   2   1

THIS SERIES IS DEDICATED TO
MASTERPIECE MINISTRIES

BUT MOSES AGAIN PLEADED, "LORD, PLEASE! SEND ANYONE ELSE."

EXODUS 4:13

1

The greatest sound in the world at the end of that summer was the jangling of the bells on the door leading into Fascination Street Records. It's the sound that brought Marvella Garcia into my life. It's the sound I hoped for on a daily basis, since the store doesn't get a lot of customers. Unfortunately, it was also the sound that introduced me to Marvel's uncle shortly before the start of the school year . . .

I'm sure the opening door is Marvel, surprising me at the store even though she's supposed to be visiting family in Michigan. But then I see a face I've seen only in passing a few times.

I know he's not looking for any kind of music. This is not the kind of guy who bothers with shopping. For *anything*. His dark brown eyes stay locked onto me as he walks up to the counter.

"What's up, Brandon?" He says it as though we've been friends for a while.

He's got a bit of a Latino accent, but at the same time he sounds like a regular Chicago guy. I just nod. I wasn't expecting to see Carlos Acosta face-to-face today. Or maybe ever.

"Look—I'm going to make this absolutely clear. I want you to leave Marvel alone. I know you'll see her at school and talk to her there. But I don't want to see you at our apartment. And I never want you speaking to my wife. Do you understand?"

I feel like someone's just come into the shop and hit me in the gut with a baseball bat. I don't know what to say. *Oh, sure, sounds great?*

Carlos Acosta wipes back his long, dark, wavy hair, the kind that looks good only on actors and musicians. He's gotta be in his thirties and he looks like he spends half the day on his appearance. I can even smell the bottle of cologne he's wearing.

"Brandon, hey—say you hear me, okay? Or I'm going to come behind that desk and force your mouth to say it."

"I hear you," I say.

There's something awful about the way he looks at me. His eyes are cold and dead. Even when he threatens me, they don't move an inch.

"The last thing I need is a six-foot-tall distraction in my life, you got that?" he says.

I nod again. He doesn't give me one last menacing glance, doesn't say anything else. He just walks back out of the store, his business apparently done.

I get my phone and tap it and see the cover photo of Marvel and me. I'm sure he waited until she was away to confront me.

The problem is that this guy doesn't know who he's talking to.

He doesn't realize that I've been threatened by worse men than him.

He also has no clue how I really feel about his niece.

Then again, she probably doesn't either. But hopefully, very soon, Marvel will know.

2

I'm sweltering in a black suit and standing outside with a bunch of people, listening to a preacher but not really hearing the words he's saying. There's no wind, and I wipe sweat off my forehead and then realize I'm dreaming. I don't own a suit like this, and I don't know who died or why all these people have gathered.

I look around for my buddies, but they're nowhere to be found. No Devon, no Frankie, none of them. Then I look for Marvel and realize this is surely her funeral, the one she's been talking about for so long.

Marvel Garcia is in a casket in a hole in the earth, and I have no idea how she died. I couldn't stop it.

I see the glassy-eyed strangers wiping tears. I see older people clutching one another in their grief. But I'm standing alone. All alone.

For a moment I stare up at the sky. It's clear and blue and so serene. I want to ask a question, call out, or just say something. But I'm speechless. And the sky is just like everybody else around me. Completely silent.

That's when I jerk awake and feel my back covered with sweat.

For a long time I think about the dream. It's not surprising, of course, not after Marvel has spent all summer sharing her conviction that she's going to die helping someone in need. How, she doesn't know. When, she doesn't know either. But she sincerely believes this is going to happen, and it's going to happen soon.

I make myself a promise once again.

It isn't going to happen, I tell myself.

She's not going to die.

Nothing is going to happen to her because I'm going to do everything I can to make sure it doesn't.

I've never longed to be some knight in shining armor or a martyr either. But I will be if that's what it takes.

I can picture Marvel in the darkness even with my eyes wide open. She's pretty much all I think about, and has been since she stepped foot into the record store at the start of the summer.

It doesn't matter what she says or believes. It doesn't matter how tough her uncle happens to be either. I just want to be at her side and know she's going to be okay.

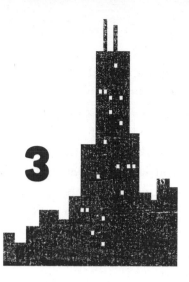

3

"I swear we have a serial killer around here."

Sometimes I really don't like the way Devon thinks. I look over at him from the sinking couch in his basement and stop playing the video game. I'm still sore from soccer practice today, especially since they've been longer and harder heading into the school year.

"Look out!" he shouts right before I'm blasted in the head. "Ouch."

"Don't freak me out any more than I am," I tell him.

"You're freaked out? Really?"

"I was working at the record store the morning they found Artie's body in the river," I remind him.

He begins guiding his character through the game and suddenly seems uninterested in the conversation.

"Are you going to start snooping around for leads on the girl from St. Charles who died?" I ask him.

"I like how you make that sound," Devon says.

"What?"

"'Snooping around.' You say it like I'm five."

"Well . . ."

"We knew Artie," Devon says. "He went to our school. And he—you know my history with him."

He doesn't say more because he's probably worried the room is bugged or someone might be spying on us through the Xbox game. Who knows? At least in Devon's mind.

I try again. "So are you going to keep sneaking around once school starts?"

Devon nods, and I notice that his hair is unusually big and wavy.

"You need a haircut," I tell him.

"This is the best boy-band hair you've ever seen," he says. "You keep yours cut way too short."

I laugh. "Because it starts looking like a mop if I don't."

"Or maybe it's because Marvel likes it that way."

Devon doesn't really even know Marvel. It's going to be interesting to have her suddenly in my life every day. And to have Devon in her life every day as well.

"She'd probably like me to grow it out, knowing her," I say.

"Yeah, she's into the seventies sort of vibe, right?"

"You look like you're going for that right now."

I watch the screen and see the first-person shooter taking out all his targets. Blood flies and heads explode and I'm not a bit shocked. We've played this game before and we're used to it.

Kids like Artie Duncan showing up dead and sliced up in the Fox River? That's something we're not used to. Yet neither of us, especially Devon, seems overly frightened by it. For Devon, it's just given him another thing to do.

I don't want to say *hobby*, but the word pops into my mind. "I'd be careful if I were you," I say to Devon.

"Oh, come on. Nothing's going to happen, especially to someone who's actually looking around to see what's up. You know? They're going to leave me alone."

I shrug and start to play the game again. "You better just hope you don't actually find something worth telling the cops about."

Devon doesn't look at me. He's not bothered in the slightest. But I am. I'm bothered because of Marvel and because of what might be coming.

I'm also bothered because Devon really, truly does need a haircut.

4

Are you there?

Absolutely not, I type.

I don't want to wake up tomorrow.

Don't you have to go to sleep to do that? I ask her.

Don't be funny.

It's going to be fine.

I didn't think I'd be this nervous.

I didn't either.

I'm being honest. These texts are just another surprising thing about this surprising girl I met a few months ago.

Maybe you should tell her about her wonderful uncle, who you just happened to meet for the first time.

But I've already decided I'm not going to say anything to Marvel about Carlos. Not now. Not yet.

I just don't want to deal with any drama, she says.

Then don't, I write. **Let it pass you by.**

It's not easy.

You've done a pretty good job with it. As far as I can see.

She remains silent.

You're pretty strong, Marvel.

Another pause. Then she writes, **Thank you. Now go to sleep.**

I smile and type, **See you in the morning.**

CANNOT WAIT!!!

I wait to see if there's anything more after the smiley face I respond with, but there's not.

Maybe I'll see her before tomorrow. Maybe Marvel will show up somewhere in my dreams.

Sleep comes and goes in what feels like a blink.

It's not even six in the morning and I'm awake. Someone might say it's because it's my last year of high school and I'm looking forward to finally graduating. Some might say it's because senior year is going to be a breeze. But the honest answer is a name. Marvella Garcia. Marvel for short.

I'm usually hard to wake up, and I'm dragging and feeling like the world is over. And I've never looked forward to school starting. But today I can't wait to get there. To find out where Marvel's locker might be. To see what classes she's in. To see her in a whole new light.

I think about texting her to see if she's up, but this, of course, is the kind of thing I *don't* want to do. To make it seem like I'm crazy about her. To show her that I think about her all the time, that I can't wait to start school to be around her more. That I'm suddenly going to be some kind of possessive boyfriend even though I'm not her boyfriend and don't own anything to be possessive about.

I don't text her because I want to give Marvel some space.

Even though, yeah, she was texting you last night.

The summer seems like some kind of strange dream. I like to replay certain moments, starting with the day she walked into my life. I replay conversations like some kind of new recording I just downloaded. I recall snapshots from scenes that I never want to forget.

Then, of course, I remember the thing that's stirring up everything, that's at the back of my mind and my heart.

"God told me I was going to go somewhere and I was going to do something special. He said I would be his instrument. He said I shouldn't be afraid, but that I would be used in an incredible way. He said I'd save others from something."

The words still seem surreal, almost silly, yet I know what she looked like when she said them.

"And then he said I would die being used in this way."

It can't happen. It shouldn't. It's one thing for a girl to watch her father kill their entire family—to have *been* there while it happened and to have been miraculously rescued from it . . . But this is too much. If God did indeed rescue her, then how and why would he allow her to die?

To save others.

Maybe this is why my heart is racing. Maybe I'm anxious to see what's about to happen. To Marvel. To us. To this thing she believes in and I fear.

The sky can fall and I'm going to stand next to you, Marvel.

That was my promise to her, and I still mean it.

This time I'll see her in rows of students instead of aisles of records. But it's not going to change a single thing.

5

She's waiting at my locker. Unfortunately, it's not the *she* I'm wanting to see.

"Hi, Taryn."

Somehow she looks even more blonde, more bright, more Taryn than I remember. She has a tan from wherever she went with her family this summer. I could have gone too, if I had been dating her. And, oh yeah, if I had wanted to suffer from permanent head and heart trauma on a daily basis.

"Look how dark you got," she says to me.

"It's a farmer's tan. That's what you get when you cut lawns instead of sit by pools."

"How are you?" she asks in her friendliest tone possible.

Her big blue eyes roam around to see who else is watching us. I'm surprised to see her here alone. Usually she has her BFFs at her side.

"Fine," I say, glancing down the hallway myself.

"You sound annoyed."

Yeah, I'd really like you to leave me alone because I'm waiting on someone.

"Just tired."

The last thing I want to do is get in an argument, especially on the first day of school.

Taryn has on tight jeans and a short little top. She brushes back her hair, clearly expecting to get the same sort of attention I used to give her. But the thing she doesn't understand is that I'm over her, that I was over her before the school year ended.

"You've been avoiding me this summer," she says.

She gives me her smile, the same sort of curve on her lips that a hook floating in water might have.

I'm about to say something, anything, to try to get her to leave so I can be alone when I see Marvel, but then it's too late. I see a dark-skinned girl in a very different outfit.

Her long, flowery skirt glides as she walks along. She's wearing a matching top that's sort of violet-colored and a massive necklace.

She walks right up to me, even though Taryn is standing there.

"I'm here," Marvel says, her smile telling me everything I need to know.

The unsure girl who texted me is gone. In her place is this confident young woman.

The look on Taryn's face is simply . . . priceless. She doesn't even try to hide it. It's like she's wondering, *Who in the world is this chick?*

"Marvel, this is Taryn," I say.

Marvel holds out her hand, but Taryn is ever the

wonderful soul I found her to be. For a moment my ex-girlfriend acts like Marvel has some hideous disease or smells bad or something. Taryn literally almost backs up, then she examines the outfit Marvel is wearing and laughs.

"Wow," Taryn says to her. "Nice outfit."

"Seven dollars. For both pieces."

Taryn looks at me with a *Really?* sort of glance. I'm embarrassed to know this rude girl.

"Love the dress," I say.

And I'm being honest. I really do.

Marvel has her dark hair in a ponytail. She looks so comfortable in her own skin, as she should.

"This is Marvel's first day," I say.

Taryn glares at me, and without even looking at Marvel again, says, "Good luck," and walks away.

I can only shake my head. "Sorry," I say to Marvel.

"Sorry for what?"

"Sorry you had to meet her right away."

"It's okay."

I keep shaking my head. "I used to go out with her."

"And now you don't." She smiles at me with a knowing look, then quickly adds, "Not that I'm saying anything's going to change."

"Change how?"

"Between you and me."

I get my books for first class and close my locker door. "Oh, come on. It's only the first day of school. Don't break up with me now."

"You can't break up with someone you're not *with*, Mr. Jeffrey."

"Okay, fine. Let's go find your locker, okay?"

"I hope I'm right next to that girl. It'll make this year extra special."

Something in her tone finally gives her away. She's a bit *too* calm and collected, and I realize she's still nervous.

"Listen, I'm going to do everything I can to make this year extra special," I tell her as we're walking.

She looks at me and drifts away a bit. "You have that look in your eye."

"What kind?"

"The same one you had all summer long."

"So?" I ask.

"Well, it's no longer summer. It's fall."

"So I'll get a new look, then."

Marvel grins. "I'm afraid that's impossible."

I laugh but I think that she's right.

The smile isn't going anywhere because the feelings producing them aren't about to change.

In fact, they might grow.

6

"Do the teachers seem nervous, or is it just me?"

I'm walking with Devon to lunch. He nods as he scans the students passing us by.

"Two of mine talked about Artie's death," Devon says. "Mrs. Schwartzburg broke down and cried."

"Oh man."

"They're more freaked out than the kids."

"Nice," I say. "Why can't adults act like—adults? You know?"

"What do you mean?"

"Be an example," I say. "Show us how to be strong or something, you know? Don't start crying."

"Wow, you're Mr. Sympathetic today."

"Maybe I'm just tired of being around my dad."

"How's he doing?"

"Nothing's changed," I say.

We enter the cafeteria, and I move away from Devon to try to find Marvel. I didn't really want to mention my father, but it slipped out.

Soon we're all sitting around Marvel, asking her questions and making her laugh. I can see others looking at us, maybe wondering who she is or why we're having a good time. Frankie can't keep his eyes off her, and Barton's loud howl is cracking me up. Obviously my buddies feel the same way I do about the new girl.

"Is Mr. Midkiff always like that?" she asks as we're talking about her science class.

"Oh, yeah," Frankie says.

"I bet he builds bombs in his basement," Barton says, rubbing his curly locks that don't look like they've seen shampoo in days.

As we're talking about the nerdy Mr. Midkiff, a group of guys approaches. A familiar square block of a head is looking my way.

"What's up, Frankie, my main man."

The voice is smug and obnoxious.

"Hey, Greg," Frankie responds without any reaction.

I've been wondering what would happen when I saw Greg Packard at school. Last year I don't think I ever even looked at the guy. Different cliques, different worlds.

Until you decided to help save a kid from getting the snot beat out of him.

"What's up, losers," Greg says to the rest of us. "So who's your girlfriend, Brando?"

"I'm Marvel," she says.

"Are you guys like a thing or something?" he asks.

The guys behind him don't say anything. They're like three bodyguards, looking around, waiting for their chance to talk and have a life.

Marvel doesn't miss a beat. "Yep. We plan to elope sometime this year."

"That's truly heartbreaking," Greg says.

She looks at me and raises her eyebrows.

"Seen your little twin around school today, Brando?"

"That's a neat little nickname," I tell him. "And no, I haven't."

I assume he's referring to Seth Belcher, the kid I kept from getting beaten up by Greg and his buddy at the beginning of summer.

Actually several times this summer.

"We have," Greg says, and glances at the meatheads with him. They all laugh.

I look at Frankie, but he's not smiling. He looks at me with an I-told-you-this-was-gonna-happen sort of glance.

They leave us there to talk about them afterward, and I wonder what happened with Seth now.

"I love jocks," Marvel says.

I nod. "You and me both."

"Hey, now, be nice," Frankie says, eating apple slices from a baggie.

"You're not a jock," she tells him.

"What category do you put me in?"

"The friend category."

"Ooh." He makes a stink face.

"What?"

"No guy wants to be called a friend," Frankie says.

"Well, Brandon's my friend." She turns to me. "Or should I call you Brando?"

I laugh. "Yes, a 'friend.' I love that term. So meaningful. But no, please don't call me Brando."

"Brando," Barton says in a loud voice that sounds like he's making a farting noise.

We all laugh, but at the back of my mind I'm still thinking about Seth.

As we're leaving the cafeteria, Frankie pulls me aside, out of earshot of Marvel.

"I told you that was going to happen," he says. "You gotta be careful."

"Come on," I say. "What's he going to do?"

"A lot. You never know with him."

"I so want to get him kicked off the football team."

Frankie gives me that look, and I reassure him. "Don't worry, I'm not going to say anything. Besides, he'll probably do it himself."

"He actually used the N-word the other day, and the coach didn't say a thing," Frankie says.

"What? To you?"

"Yeah. Joking, of course. But it wasn't so funny."

"That guy's an idiot."

"Pretty good football player, though."

"Football's not everything."

Frankie smiles. "It's almost everything."

He slides up beside Marvel and slips his arm around her. Then he tells her about the big play he made last year in a championship football game. If I didn't know him I'd be jealous, but that's just Frankie. Marvel listens attentively, acting like it's the greatest story she's ever heard.

She glances at me and smiles.

It's nice to have her in my world.

7

"You don't have to take me home, you know."

I look over at Marvel and smile. "Yes I do. Didn't you read your school handbook? Page forty-three."

"Really? I haven't gotten that far."

"Look—we don't have soccer practice today, since the coach killed us this past week. I won't always be able to take you home like this."

I'm still getting used to driving the Honda Pilot, a ridiculously generous thank-you gift from my boss at the record store for working for free over the summer. Both Marvel and I are still technically working there, though I'm not sure how many hours we'll have now that school has started. I could use another job since I won't be cutting lawns much longer.

"So how was it?" I ask. "Your first day."

"Interesting."

"Yeah? How so?"

"Well, I ran into your girlfriend several more times, and

each time she made a point of singling me out to her friends and then laughing or being very petty."

"That's Taryn. My *ex*."

"Yeah, she's quite . . . quite a girl."

I laugh. "Don't judge me for being with her."

"She's pretty."

I glance over at Marvel.

No, you're the pretty one, pretty in the places a girl should be, inside and out.

"What?" she says.

I shake my head. "Nothing."

"So two guys asked me out."

"What? Really?"

She nods. Then I wait. And wait. And wait a little longer.

"So?" I finally have to ask.

"What?"

"What'd you say?"

She gives me a funny look. "Seriously?"

I'll take that as a no.

"Met some nice people. And some not-so-nice people. I think it'll be a good year."

"Glad we have English together. Maybe we can study together."

"Maybe you have an ulterior motive."

"Oh, I totally do."

She looks my way and I know—I can just tell—this girl likes me. It makes me want to bring it up again, her resistance and her belief in this big, huge thing about to happen and the reality of whatever she's thinking about. But I don't.

"You know, Brandon—"

"No, wait." I interrupt so fast she's a bit surprised.

"What?"

"Just don't—don't add to that."

"To what?"

"Just—I know what you're going to say."

"You do?" Her smile fills her whole face, as if her ears and nose are somehow grinning too. It's cute.

"Yes, of course, and just . . . just don't."

"You don't want me to talk?"

I laugh and turn into the apartment complex where she lives. "I just don't want to give up."

"Aww."

She pats my arm in a sweet way. I know she means well.

"Thank you for the ride," she says.

I nod. It's not like I had any sort of notion of going inside. The closest I've ever gotten is seeing the door open and meeting her aunt. But I'm not going anywhere close to her aunt or her apartment, not after my nice little conversation with Uncle Carlos. But still—I was kind of hoping to stay and talk. About something. Anything.

"Did you, uh, see anything at school today? You know—anything weird?"

The dark eyes look at me, through me. Suddenly I see a trace of sadness in them. She shakes her head. "No. Thankfully. Did you?"

"Me? No. Not at all."

"Good," Marvel says. "Then that means that school is safe."

"Yeah. But there's home and work and Appleton and the rest of the world to wonder about."

"Yeah."

We don't say anything more. I guess there's nothing more to say.

"Talk later?"

I nod, not sure if it's a statement or a question or just a farewell phrase.

I guess I'll find out when later comes.

8

Fascination Street Records is a ghost town. It's only five in the evening but still—if I was Harry, I'd probably be a bit nervous about the lack of store traffic. Or the lack of any kind of activity besides the vibrating speakers belting out the moody music he's playing. I'm here to check on my hours for the upcoming week.

I see Harry pop out from the back room, his curly hair even wilder than usual. He's wearing a new pair of glasses, the cool kind that say, *Yeah sure, my eyesight's going, but I can still look trendy.*

"Wow, I actually thought we had a customer."

"Sorry to disappoint," I say. "I can buy something if you want."

"Nah, buddy, that's fine. How are you doing?"

"Good. I just came in to see my hours."

"I only have you down for Saturday. Marvel and you."

I look for myself to see if he's kidding, but he's not. "That's cool."

Harry nods and yawns. He looks a little more tired than usual. Maybe I just woke him up from a nap.

"How was school?" he asks.

"Fine."

"On a scale of one to ten, how intense are things there? You know, with the deaths of Artie and the St. Charles girl."

"Maybe a seven, maybe more, depending on the teacher."

"Higher is worse?" Harry asks.

I nod.

"Well, just make sure you don't suddenly let down your guard."

Harry has talked to me like this before. Like a father might talk to his son. Which is good, because there's no way Dad is going to do it.

I look around, wanting to change the subject. "Who's this?"

"The Eagles. Before your time."

"I've heard of them."

Harry laughs. "Saw a documentary on them recently and figured I'd dust off the old records. So tell me. How is la señorita doing today?"

This was a nickname that Harry would occasionally call Marvel. She'd always laugh at it, and I don't think he ever meant it to sound bad. It was one of those terms of affection or endearment or whatever they're called.

"She's doing well."

"You guys still a thing?"

"No, we're not a thing," I say. "We've never been a thing."

I want to tell him it's complicated, but that sounds so clichéd. The truth is exactly that, however.

"She's into you, I know that. I think those tickets to Lollapalooza helped."

"If we get married, I'm *so* going to invite you."

Harry's eyes study me from behind his glasses. He looks humored, as if I'm missing some big joke.

"What?"

"Can I tell you something?"

"Absolutely not," I say.

"No, seriously. Girls like Marvel, or my wife—they're rare in this world. They don't come around much. And when they do, you gotta chase after them."

I want to tell him that's exactly what I've been doing since the day she stepped foot into his store.

"That's what I did with Sarah. I chased after her even when she kept turning me down."

"Don't they call that stalking?" I ask.

Harry laughs. "I was patient. I wasn't harassing her or anything. But I could tell. She was into me. Like Marvel is into you."

"I think you need to remind her of this when you see her next."

"Guys can't tell girls what to do. That's an unspoken rule. Learn that now and you'll be way ahead of the game."

It takes me a very long time to drive home, and I know the reason why.

I'm still afraid of what I might find when I get there.

Maybe Dad will be clean and sober for ten years and I'll learn to trust him, but not yet. It's only been a few weeks since our father-and-son outing. The one where his drunken "drive-on" madness was followed by a hit-and-run out of nowhere.

I still don't know who hit us, but the rear-end collision probably saved us from a much worse accident.

Maybe it was my guardian angel taking things to a new level. Or maybe it was Dad's drinking buddy who was really peeved that Dad hadn't invited *him* on a midnight drunken drive.

When I open the door to our house, I smell something strange. Something cooking. Dinner?

I go into the kitchen and see Mom there, home early, working over the stove. A very strange sight, especially on a weeknight.

"How'd the first day go?"

She's still in her work clothes, wearing a new outfit that I haven't seen—a dressy skirt and heels.

"Well?" she asks.

"Good," I say.

"Oh, stop."

"What?"

"Don't act so shocked to see your mother cooking."

"Well . . ."

"I wanted to celebrate you boys' first day."

I nod.

Wonder how Dad's going to be celebrating?

We talk for a few minutes about nothing—school and classes—and then I head upstairs to my room. No father-spotting, which is a good thing.

My brothers are in the game room playing a video game. No surprise. I don't go in there. I'll see them soon enough. Instead I go into my room and text Marvel.

About to have a family sit-down dinner. Feeling a bit freaked out. Not sure how this happened.

I wait for a reply, but none comes. Soon my mom calls out for us.

I breathe in and close my eyes. I hear Alex and Carter tramping down the stairs.

They don't know the truth. Neither does Mom.

I let out a long breath, maybe a sigh. Then I open my eyes and look out my window. I wish there was a tree next to it. Then I'd open the window and crawl down and get far, far away from this place.

But I'm stuck. This is home, and there's nothing I can do about it.

9

Mom used to talk about how good-looking Dad was back in college when they met. I've sort of forgotten those comments since Dad started drinking too much and pounding on me now and then. But as I sit down at the table and actually look at him, I can see it. At one point in his life he could have been decent looking. He's shaved, for one thing, and it looks like he's gotten a haircut, which is another. He doesn't look so hard, either.

"Hello, Brandon," he says.

I say hi and look away.

Hearing him say my name just isn't a pleasant thing.

There's something else that's different. Dad is wearing clothes I've never seen him in. He doesn't look like he woke up in the garbage dump.

Soon all five of us are sitting around eating pot roast. I can't really remember the last time we sat at the table, eating a meal together. And whenever that might have been, we sure weren't eating pot roast.

"Didn't your mother outdo herself?" Dad says as he looks at her and smiles.

What house am I in, and what'd they do to my parents?

The way the two of them look at each other . . . it's kinda weird.

"This really is good, LeeAnn."

I notice the glass of Diet Coke in front of him. I haven't seen Dad take a drink since the night he almost killed both of us. Mom has said he's going to meetings. So yeah, maybe this will be the rest of our lives. Pot roast and Diet Cokes and my parents making eyes at each other. As for those slaps and punches and hateful words, we'll just sweep those under the rug or wherever they can go.

"So how is soccer going?" Dad asks.

"Same as always."

You do know soccer is the round ball, as opposed to that oval thing you throw?

Both Mom and Dad look at me. Maybe my reply was a bit strong.

"When's your next game?" Mom asks.

This is funny. Really funny.

Suddenly my parents have decided to show up at the dinner table and in my life. Sure, it's my senior year of high school, but better late than never, right?

If Dad really cared, he'd know that I'm a very average player who rarely even thinks about the sport. The fury of my father's support for the Chicago Bears/Blackhawks/Bulls has affected my attitude toward them.

"We have a soccer game this Thursday," I say, hoping it's way too soon for them to commit to go to.

"That would work for me," Mom tells Dad.

I laugh as I see them looking at each other again, making plans I don't know about regarding my life, making it clear I'm still not in the same room as them.

For a second—a split second, but I see it—Dad gives me a look. A familiar look, one I know and recognize oh so well. The smile is briefly off his face and the anger is back.

Watch out, boy.

That's what it tells me.

He almost says something, but my middle brother beats him to it.

"Are you guys coming to a game?" Alex asks. "Can I stay after to watch it?"

"We are," Mom says. "About time, huh? It was your father's idea."

I look at her and force a smile.

What if I told you it was his idea to slam a vodka bottle over my head?

I see him cut his meat with a knife, slowly and carefully. He gives me another short, serious look.

"You can watch only if Brandon scores," Dad says to Alex.

"Soccer's boring," says Carter. He's the youngest and the gift to the sports gods.

Sometimes I just want to punch his face. Not figuratively, but literally. His pretty face that's probably going to break all the girls' hearts.

"What do you say? Think you can do that for your brother?"

I look at Dad. The statement seems like a challenge.

"I'll score one for each of you," I say. "How's that sound?"

My reply sounds like a dare.

So you're coming to my game, I'll show you. I'll show you there's skill and talent in this thing called soccer. I'll show you that you don't have to tackle people or throw them a ball to be a good player.

"We just want to see you play," Mom says.

But I don't buy it. I don't buy that Dad suddenly wants to watch me play soccer. He's ridden me for years for not being his quarterback-in-waiting. He's been angry that I haven't been a diehard Bears fan and that I actually sorta hate them because I sorta hate him.

I don't buy the soccer game and I don't buy the Diet Coke and I really don't buy this whole thing.

But as I have done for seventeen years, I'll go with this. I'll sit here and eat my food and not say a thing. Especially to Mom. I can't imagine the pain and the hurt inside her if she knew everything. That's one of the biggest reasons why I've never stood my ground.

I've kept things from her for long enough. Just a little longer and I'm gone.

"Is *Marvel* going to be there?" Alex asks me.

Now he's the one I want to pound. I don't even acknowledge the question.

"And who is Marvel?" asks Dad.

"His Mexican girlfriend," Carter says with a laugh. Seriously.

"So she's your girlfriend?" Mom asks me.

"You're believing a twelve-year-old?"

A dark gray cloud seems to hover over Dad as he gives me a grim look.

Yeah, Marvel's uncle isn't the only one who doesn't want me around her.

"I saw you with her today," Alex says. "A couple times."

"She works at the record store," I say. "She's just a friend."

Dad's still looking at me.

Yeah, that's right, I remember. I remember your words the night you slammed the bottle against my skull.

I look back at him.

"You stay away from her. You got that? Her kind only attracts trouble."

"Well, I hope we get to meet her," Mom says.

Dad doesn't say anything. But I know. I know for a fact that he hasn't changed. I can feel the anger and the intensity and the hate just bubbling inside. I can see it too. The others can't, and that's okay. I've seen it before and I've seen what he's done with it.

"Three goals, yeah right," Carter says.

I'll show them. Even if it's difficult to score *one* goal in a game.

I don't care.

I'll show *him*.

10

If I were my own older brother, I'd do something about Dad. I would. I wouldn't let him pick on me. I would stand up for, well, me. The same way I stood up to the football morons picking on Seth this past summer. The same way I want to stand up to whoever (or whatever) Marvel is going to be dealing with when the time comes. If the time ever comes.

As the TV show I'm watching ends and I think about the homework I still have to do, I get a text from Devon.

Got a weird text just now. Sorta freaked out.

From who? What's it say?

Here . . .

I wait for a minute.

"Hey, Devon. Just checking in to see if you need anything since Artie's no longer around. A friend."

I get goose bumps. I reread it several times.

I know the *need anything* isn't referring to friendship or playing video games. It still blows my mind a bit that Devon bought pot from Artie, especially since I've never considered Devon a pothead.

A friend? What's that mean? Who's it from?

I just have a number, Devon replies.

You should tell the cops.

No way. Tell them what? I bought drugs from Artie?

Can't you tell the cops something?

Like what?

I'm not sure what to think. Is someone that stupid, to text Devon asking if he needs anything? And *does* Devon need something? Does he want more pot?

Did you answer the text? I ask.

Not yet.

I think of Devon snooping around and telling me how he thinks this weirdo old guy Otis Sykes might have had something to do with Artie's death.

All I know is that nobody should be snooping around into anything to do with Artie's death, *especially* since that girl from St. Charles was found.

Tell him you're fine and leave things be, I text Devon.

Why? What if I really want some?

I laugh. **Then find a new dealer.**

I'm just curious.

I wouldn't be curious. I'd stay away. Seriously.

What if it has something to do with Artie's death?

I can't believe how flippant Devon can be.

You really want to find out? You're crazy.

It just seems like it'd be cool to not just be a role player in some video game. You know?

Devon's last message seems to hover there.

Yeah, sure, but in a video game you can die multiple times. In the real world you get one life.

Leave it to others to figure out Artie's death, I text him.

No reply, so I text him again.

Seriously, Devon.

Yeah, yeah.

Maybe this has nothing to do with anything except someone trying to sell some pot. Hey—they've made it legal in some states, right?

But Artie was found in the river not just dead but seriously dead—like messed-up-all-over dead.

The drug thing has to factor into this somehow.

I know one thing about Devon—he does his own thing. I doubt I'll be able to change his mind.

And I can't personally try to protect both him and Marvel at the same time.

11

The second day of school, I walk by Marvel's locker several times, and finally I just wait. But she never shows up.

During first period I feel like throwing up. I swear— nothing like this has happened. Like ever. Even the stuff with my father doesn't compare. That fear and dread are nothing like having a real and aching worry over someone else.

Then, in the few minutes between first and second periods, I feel something else: peace.

All from seeing her smile.

"Good morning," she says.

Something finally releases out of the clogged-up dam inside my soul.

"Are you okay?"

She nods. I don't even notice what she's wearing. I'm just looking into her eyes and seeing the curves of her smile.

"Of course."

Something rushes into the protected place residing in my heart.

"Good."

And yes. For now, for this morning, it's good.

After school I swing past Marvel's locker on my way to practice. Our first game is two days away. The one where my parents are going to come and hold hands and maybe make out in the stands. The one in which, in a moment of insanity, I vowed to score three goals. I decide to tell Marvel about it.

"Hey—you know I have a soccer game this Thursday."

"Is that where they throw the ball or kick it?" she asks me with a smile.

Her locker is open, and I can see the black floppy hat she wore to school. It's too big and obnoxious to be worn in the classroom, but I love the fact that she wore it to school anyway.

"My parents are coming to it," I say. "Both of them."

"Is that a bad thing?"

I give her an *Are you crazy?* look.

"What?"

"Yeah, it's a bad thing. I don't want them there. My brother is coming too."

"So do you want me to meet them?"

I laugh. "No, not really."

"That's not very nice."

"My father is not very nice," I tell her.

She already knows the truth, and her face gets serious. "I'll be there if you want me to."

"I told them I'd score three goals."

"Why's that?"

"I don't know. 'Cause I'm an idiot."

"Well then, score three goals."

She grabs her books and starts to head toward the door.

"Bye then," I call out.

She doesn't look back but only waves with her fingers. I stand there, wanting to follow her, knowing I'm looking and acting a bit desperate.

Later that night I get a text from her.

Romans 12:12 gives me lots of comfort. I find myself going back to it again and again: "Rejoice in our confident hope. Be patient in trouble, and keep on praying."

I'm not sure what to say except **Thanks.**

Then, before I can think of anything else, she sends another message.

Don't worry about the game or your parents. You'll do great.

I exhale. **I don't know.**

Yeah you do. I think you know quite well.

And how do you know this? I ask.

Because I notice things. And I've noticed lots of things about YOU.

Uh-oh.

No, she writes. **Don't be worried. I'm the one who needs to be worried.**

Why is that?

Because I like the things I notice.

I smile as I read her message. I want to tell her to just give in, then. Give me a chance. Just let things happen and put on her wide-brim hat and hold my hand and let whatever happens *happen*.

Forget yourself and forget your uncle and forget what you think is going to happen in the future and focus on the now.

See you tomorrow, she says before I can type any kind of adequate response.

Good night.

I think of this girl, this bright light coming from such a dark place. I know that the things she believes about God and the Bible and hope and all that are very real to her. They're not nice sayings on Twitter just to fill a box. They're the things she truly believes.

I'm not sure I'm ready to rejoice, and I'm not quite ready to pray.

The cool thing is that Marvel knows this. She knows this and doesn't seem to mind.

12

That Thursday starts with a not-so-pleasant sight. Mom is already gone and I'm getting ready for school, going through the typical motions. I finish a box of cereal, so I decide to be a good son and put the box in recycling. That's when I see it. The top of a bottle that doesn't look like Mountain Dew. I bend over into the large recycling can and pull up a clear bottle. A vodka bottle.

Unless Carter or Alex is starting to sip some of this in his sleep, there's only one person it could belong to.

I put it back in the container and make sure it's out of view. I'm angry but I'm not surprised.

I don't say anything to anyone, not even Marvel. The nagging, irritating, awful thoughts come back like some kind of lunch I packed for myself at home. I want to just throw them all away, but I can't. It's not that easy.

I don't listen to my teachers and don't do anything, really. I just keep wondering what's going to happen at home. When Dad's going to snap again.

And he for sure will snap again.

I'm not worried about myself. He can beat me up again, whatever. It's Mom and Alex and Carter I'm worried about. And what if something goes from bad to worse?

What if he's a news report waiting to happen, the same way Marvel's father was? The same way Artie Duncan was?

Bad things happen to good people. Awful people do things to nice people.

At lunchtime, I don't say much while the guys talk to Marvel like always. She eventually picks up on it and asks me what's wrong, but I say nothing.

I really want to be left alone.

Marvel, in her usual unbelievable way of reading my mind and my soul, does exactly that.

I'm lost in my own world between classes when I see Seth Belcher. At first I don't recognize him 'cause he's got a Mohawk. As he passes me it suddenly clicks, and I say hey.

He just nods, so I turn and follow him.

"Seth, hey man. Hey—how's it going?"

"Fine."

"How's your week been?"

"The same as always."

He has no expression or emotion.

"People leaving you alone?"

Again he gives a nod. I'm still walking with him, heading the opposite direction I'm supposed to go.

"Well, okay, cool."

I don't know what else to say, so I stop and he keeps going.

Why do I even bother trying?

Maybe the guy just needs a friend. Or a hug. Or a girlfriend.

I'd like to say I feel better for reaching out to him, but I don't.

The field is wet, because at some point this afternoon it rained. It sorta fits my day and my mood and the fact that I'm probably not going to score even one goal tonight.

I realize that the whole finding-the-vodka-in-the-garbage really wrecked me for some reason. So before going out on the field, I have a pep talk with myself. Because this feeling sorry for myself just doesn't cut it.

You knew he was just faking it to begin with, so why are you so surprised?

Maybe that's true, but I did have some bit of hope. A tiny wish that maybe, just maybe, Dad had changed.

He's not going to touch Mom because he knows better. And he's not going to hurt Alex or Carter. They're not strong enough.

I believe this. But I'm still afraid for them.

Take this anger and do something with it. Burn it out on the field. Show him.

It's what I've already done for as long as I can remember. I've worked hard and played hard and tried to do something with this feeling, with the knowledge that there's nothing I can do about him.

I see Mom talking to Alex, and Dad waiting right by the stands. It's still overcast and wet. I walk over to where Dad stands.

I can feel the anger inside of me wanting to do something, anything.

"I know about the vodka," I tell him, looking him square

in the eyes. "They don't know, but I do. You're not faking anything with me."

For a moment I see his hard stare. I'm sure there are things he wants to say, but for now he's quiet.

I head to the field.

I'm going to show him. I'm going to show him that I'm better than this and better than him and that I'm special regardless of how awful he might make me feel.

This is my chance to shine.

13

Five minutes into the game, I know I'm doomed. It's not just that I'm trying way too hard, but there's a freshman player on the other team who thinks this game is football or something. He's short, but he's got the body of a tank. Short but stubby. Like a block that moves around and takes the ball away from me. A big block that also trips me up and elbows me and bangs its head against mine.

I receive a long pass from a midfielder and am in range for a good true shot when the ball is taken away by Stubby in spectacular fashion. The kid is really good. This angers me, of course, so I follow him and try to get the ball by kicking from behind. I take him down and wind up with a yellow card.

I see something in his eyes. Something that says, *You better not do that again.*

Five minutes later Stubby gets a yellow card by trying to kick the ball and launching a foot squarely in my shin. As if planned, I go tumbling and the pain kills and the referee holds up the yellow and tells us to knock it off.

By halftime I'm still without a single goal. I don't bother looking at the stands. This is crazy. I'm frustrated and ignore the coach when he tells me to just shake it off. I don't want to shake anything off. Not Stubby the defender and not my father and not anything.

Twice I almost score, working my way around Stubby now that I know his tricks. But I don't do myself any favors by trying to pull some kind of amazing shot, and instead launch the soccer ball ten feet above the goal.

I know I'm getting under Stubby's skin. The score is still zero to zero.

I have the ball and I'm dribbling down the side of the field when he comes crashing into me like some kind of lineman.

Hey, Stubby, you been talking to Greg the bullying football player by any chance?

We both go down and go down hard. I twist my ankle, and for a second I think I might be injured. Seriously injured.

As I get up on my hands and knees I feel a kick in my back.

I seriously just got kicked in the back.

I don't even hesitate. I launch myself at Stubby.

The whistle goes off and some other players come around us and it's a bit blurry for a second. All I know is that within two seconds I'm on top of Stubby, and I literally feel like taking my fist and ramming it up his nose.

I'm about to do this when I happen to glance at the stands. Just for a split second.

And no, it's not my father I see. I don't get a glimpse of the man I'm suddenly acting like.

I see just one figure.

Marvel. Standing in the bleachers. She's smiling, for some strange reason.

The sky above us is suddenly brighter.

Wasn't it just overcast?

Nobody else is around. It's just the two of us on this field.

This happened when we went to Lollapalooza. For a moment, the world disappeared.

I blink and then suddenly life turns gray again and I see a square face lunging at me, and then I feel my shirt being pulled by one of my teammates.

Then I see the red card coming out and know I'm done for the day.

Strangely, I'm no longer angry. Not for the moment. I'm confused, wondering what happened and where I went and why I did what I did.

"What did your parents say?" Marvel asks me an hour later when she climbs into the SUV next to me.

"Mom tried to encourage me. Dad said nothing."

"Not a word?"

I shake my head. "No. He's surely ticked off. That's when he's the most quiet. When he's raging inside. At least—the most quiet around Mom."

"I'm sorry."

I shake my head and start the car. "No. I was being stupid. That kid was a good player. I was trying too hard."

"Maybe I shouldn't have come."

"No," I say. "It's not you. It's my parents. It's just . . ."

There's so much to say, and I'm not exactly sure how to say it. I just shake my head again.

"At least you guys won."

"Yeah. The team played better without me."

"They might have been playing *for* you," Marvel says.

As a light in the dark, this girl next to me.

For a second I think of what happened, what I saw or imagined I saw right as I was going to punch the kid on the field in the face.

"You know—I swear I . . ."

"You what?" Marvel asks.

I don't know how to come right out and ask it. I'll sound completely mad. I know it.

Of course she's the one you saw, the only one you saw. In your mind.

"It's nothing." I stare ahead and see the houses of Appleton passing by.

This isn't the same sort of thing that happened at Lollapalooza with Marvel.

"You sure?"

"Yeah."

I have my window open since it's a warm September evening. I suddenly find myself wanting to just drive and keep driving. To not drop her off and not go home.

"Let's run away," I say.

"Okay," Marvel says, not missing a beat.

She's wearing the wide hat with the floppy brim. She really is a beautiful sight sitting right next to me. A glamorous movie star, and I'm her chauffeur.

"I don't know. How far away is Key West?"

"Key West?" Marvel asks. "Why there?"

"Why not? Sounds warm. And far away."

"We can do better than Key West."

"Come on—it's like the farthest point south," I say.

"We might not have enough gas."

"I can get more."

"Where will we stay?" she asks with a tone of mock concern. "How will we survive?"

"I'll find a job on the beach picking up coconuts."

"Coconuts?" She laughs. "I don't think there are coconuts in Key West."

"Then mangoes. Or oranges. Or whatever. Doesn't matter. I'll pick them up."

"How about Canada?" Marvel says. "Find a mountain lodge somewhere."

"That'll do," I say.

"You can grow a beard and cut down trees for the fireplace, and we can eat deer and elk."

"Might be a problem," I say.

"What?"

"I can't quite grow a beard."

She laughs.

Already I'm in a better mood. As usual. The game and my parents seem so far away, like the rest of life.

"I don't want to drop you off," I tell her when we are parked in the lot in front of her apartment building.

"So you want to stay in the car all night?"

I nod. "Yes. Absolutely."

"What about homework?"

"It can wait."

"What about brushing your teeth? I have to brush my teeth and wash my face before bed. Must."

"I'd still like you with bad breath and an oily face."

Marvel cracks up. "You can be quite adorable, Brandon Jeffrey."

"That's me."

"When you're not tackling people on the soccer field."

"Hey," I say. "He kicked me."

"Oh yeah, but still."

I think about home for a moment and about what awaits me.

Maybe Dad'll tackle me when I come through the front door. Or maybe Marvel's uncle will see me from the window right now and come rushing down.

"I should go."

I want to ask Marvel a hundred questions. Or at least one really big one.

Where are we headed? Is all this going somewhere?

"I see that look in your eyes," she says.

"What look?"

"*That* look. I can't explain it."

I want to put my arm around her or hold her hand. I want to give her a kiss. Just one.

"I'd ask what you're thinking, but I think I might know," she says.

"I'm sure you know."

"You know what I'm thinking as well, right? The things we've talked about?"

I nod, but I don't want to think about it. I don't want to go back there. I don't want to turn on that song because I'm hoping there's another one to play.

I want to change your mind.

"I know, I know," I say.

"Please. Don't get angry."

I nod. I should be happy. I've got this amazing girl who's become an amazing friend, and that should be enough.

Yeah right, Brando.

I feel her take my hand and squeeze it. "Next time you'll score."

For a second I'm wondering if she's talking about on the soccer field or in the car.

I say good night and tell her to text me later. If she's bored. Or if she's not.

14

I'm home and in my room thinking about Marvel when the door opens and Mom appears, wearing her pajamas and robe and looking ready for bed.

"You doing okay?" she asks as she walks in and then closes the door behind her.

"Wonderful," I say.

"Don't worry. I'm not coming in here to talk about the game."

"What game? That was a mess out there."

Mom smiles. "I met Marvel," she says. "What a beautiful girl."

I nod. "Yeah."

"She really seemed sweet."

"She really is."

"You should have her over for dinner sometime."

I shrug. "We're not together or anything. We're just friends."

"Sure."

"No, really. That's the way she wants it."

"She could still have dinner with us if she wanted to."

"That'd be a bit odd. Even if we were together."

Mom looks at me and seems serious, like she's going to say something deep and profound and heavy.

"Maybe one day a dinner with the family won't feel so odd."

I nod.

You don't want to know, Mom.

"Next time you'll score some goals," Mom tells me.

I know she's just trying to encourage me.

"Yeah, maybe. Thanks."

"Good night."

A few moments after she leaves, I'm thinking about texting Marvel when she beats me to it.

You inspired a blog.

I smile. **You have a blog?**

Yeah.

I wait for more and then ask, **Well, do I get to see it?**

Okay. Here's the link.

I open it up on my computer, and sure enough, she's got a page called *Final Thoughts*. It's got a simple design and only two posts up so far. I'm not sure I really love the name, but I'll try to not think too hard about it. I start to read the latest post.

IN THE THICK

Tangible this thing I can't touch.
Tolerable the desires that make my heart rush.
I feel weakness for my wondering.
I feel wounded for my inactions.

I know what is right, what is good, what is meant to be.
But I want the wrong so badly.
My soul stirs toward the skies, toward my Father who watches
    over me.
Yet my skin seeks solace in the night.
I try. And keep trying.
I stay the course. So lost in the thick.

The image on the blog is fog with sunlight trying to come through it. I stare at the picture and then reread the blog.

Desires?

Want the wrong?

Skin seeks solace?

I wonder if she's talking about me. If somehow I'm a small or big part of this blog.

She did say you inspired it.

I text her back.

That was beautiful.

Thanks, she says. Short and sweet.

That's pretty deep.

I can go there sometimes.

I hesitate to ask her this but can't help it. **Am I part of the wrong?**

There's a pause, then, **Yes.**

I don't mean to be.

You don't do anything. It's just—I know what I've been called to do.

Do you think that can change? I ask.

No. Maybe but—I don't think so.

But I think so. I believe that maybe it can change.

And maybe I can help change it.
This blog post sounded sorta sad, I text.
It is.
I'm sorry.
Don't be, Marvel writes. **I'm glad to have a friend like you.**
Yeah, me too.
I gotta go. Just wanted to make sure you saw that.
Thanks, I tell her. **See you tomorrow.**
Bye!

I keep the page open on my laptop for a long time. And the more I read it, the more it makes me happy. This girl likes me. She likes me a whole lot. Why? I'm not sure. Surely not for my soccer skills or for my ability to stand up to people like my father. Maybe I just—maybe it doesn't even matter. She likes me and is struggling because she wants to be more than friends.

I think of the stupid statement I made about scoring three goals. That same sort of feeling is inside of me right now. An angry sort of determination.

I'm not letting you go.
So there.
I'm going to be at your side to help you get through this.
So there.
And one day you're not going to call me your weakness.
I close my laptop but still feel Marvel very much by my side.

15

I wake up Friday morning determined to ask Marvel out and not accept a *no*. But as soon as I walk into school Devon corners me at my locker.

"Hey—we're on for tonight," he tells me in a whisper.

It's funny to see Devon whispering, since usually he talks as if he's thinking to himself—which means he can sometimes talk very loud while looking at the open sky. But now he's got his lips tight together and anybody who looked at him would stare harder since he looks so silly, especially with his big mound of hair looming like a mushroom on his head.

"Stop being goofy," I tell him. "What are you talking about?"

"The—you know. The transaction. We're on."

"Tonight? We?"

"Yes," he mumbles, only it comes out like *Yer*.

"Okay, why are you talking like that? Are you being watched?"

"You don't know."

I close my locker and look around. Yeah, I'm pretty sure I know we're not being watched.

"Didn't I tell you it was a bad idea?" I ask him.

"I don't recall hearing that," he says, not looking at me.

"And you want me to come?"

"Safety in numbers," he says.

Maybe the first sensible thing he's said.

"What time?"

He stares at the ceiling. The *ceiling*. As if Big Brother is watching us now.

"I'm going to get a text. Want to just come over tonight? Got plans?"

I shake my head. "No, that sounds good."

I'll figure out another time to ask Marvel out. Another time for her to possibly say no.

Tonight I will babysit Devon and try to persuade him never to do this again. Maybe tonight will convince him that there's nothing there that needs investigating.

At least I hope there isn't.

"Hey," Devon says as I turn to walk to class.

"Yeah."

"You got cash?"

"I'm not buying you drugs."

"Shhhhhhh."

He looks around and seriously attracts more attention. A group of freshmen girls are walking toward us and he backs into one.

"Devon, man—seriously, chill."

I'm glad to see Marvel, but I can tell by the look on her face that something is wrong.

"You okay?"

Her dark eyes look bright but troubled. She doesn't say yes or no or anything.

"Marvel."

Her eyes tear up, and I bend down to look her square in the face.

"Hey—what's up?"

"I . . . I got another—"

She closes her mouth and then shuts her eyes too.

"Hey—what? You got another what?"

"Another sign. Another message. Another nudge."

I nod. This time I'm the one looking around to see if anybody is watching. But nobody is.

"What happened? Did you have a dream?"

Marvel shakes her head. "No."

"Then what?"

"I heard something last night that woke me up. It sounded like—like someone screaming. I thought it was my aunt. I thought—well, I didn't know if my aunt and uncle were arguing or something. But they were asleep."

"What was it?"

She starts to head to her next class. I don't care if I'm late for mine. I don't care about anything for the moment.

"It was coming from outside my hallway. And I was scared. It was a girl crying, shouting out, screaming. And it was like I was the only one who could hear it. So I just waited and waited for it to go away but it wouldn't. So I finally opened the door."

Suddenly Marvel starts to shake. I stop her and pull her over in a small area at the end of a set of lockers.

"It's okay."

"No, it's not okay," she says. "I saw a girl lying down in the hallway, screaming. Holding her chest. She was bleeding. Her hand was all bloody."

Tears are falling down her face now, and I'm trying to shield her from anybody who might see this.

"It's okay. Did you call for help?"

She shakes her head, then laughs like a crazy person.

"No."

"You didn't? Why? What was wrong?"

"The girl crying, screaming out in pain. She was me."

I wait for something more, for some kind of explanation, for anything. But none comes. She wipes her eyes and says she has to go and that we'll talk later.

For the next two classes before lunch, all I can think of is three words.

She was me.

16

Sometimes I swear I'm being watched.

It must be Devon rubbing off on me, 'cause I don't actually see anybody the way I did in the past, like the time I was mowing lawns and a car parked and seemed to watch me for a while. Or the time I saw someone in the shadows following me. Could it have been the same person who did that awful thing to Artie? To the St. Charles girl? They still haven't confirmed the two are linked, but it makes sense.

It's not quite dark and nobody is around, but I still feel watched as I walk the couple of blocks to Devon's house.

Maybe you're nervous 'cause you're about to go buy drugs.

But I'm not really that nervous. It's not like I'm buying it for me. It's not like I'm nervous about getting caught.

What about being nervous for what might happen next?

No, it's none of those things.

The evening is warm and I can hear cars in the background and birds chirping. Someone is playing loud music. Another house has its garage door open and someone is in there working on a car. Just another day in suburbia. Nothing to worry about.

I reach the edge of the sidewalk at an intersection and stop. I turn around and study all the houses around me. The streets lining them. The trees and the parkways.

There's nothing strange. Nobody peeking out.

Yet behind every shut window and closed door is a story. Maybe even a secret or two.

The only question is which door will open, and what secret will come spilling out of it.

"Tell me something. Have we been here before?"

We're still sitting in Devon's Jeep 'cause I told him to wait a minute. The car is in darkness; the glow from the one lone streetlamp doesn't reach us.

"I haven't," Devon answers. "You go on drug runs by yourself?"

"No. This house. Doesn't it look familiar?"

He shakes his head. His hair looks more massive than ever, like you could hide a small animal inside of it.

"Remember that night we drove Seth 'home,' except it wasn't to his house, it was a friend's house? Well, *that's* the house."

Devon just laughs, and I ask him what's so funny.

"Hey, man—when you need to score, you need to score."

"Stop trying to sound all gangster and such."

"It's 'gangsta' and no, I'm not talking that. You sure we came here?"

"I'm sure."

"Come on, let's go get it and then get out of here."

We get out of the car, and I follow Devon. He's wearing a long overcoat that looks a bit shady.

"Where'd you get that coat?" I ask him.

"Outlet mall."

It looks like it might have belonged to his grandfather, but knowing Devon bought it, I'm assuming it probably cost a couple of hundred bucks. He looks like he could hide a shotgun underneath it.

We get to the front door and don't see a light on anywhere.

"I hope this is the right place," Devon says.

"This is the address."

He presses the doorbell, but we don't hear anything.

"You think it works?"

I shrug. Devon knocks on the door once, then again a little harder.

"You sure you have the right date and time?" I ask him.

"Yeah."

I get that weird feeling again of being watched. This house is at the end of the street, so there's no house on one side. The house on the other side seems dark and abandoned.

Sorta like this one.

I turn around and look out at the street and Devon's Jeep.

"I don't know about this."

I think about Artie Duncan, the student they found dead in the Fox River. All cut up with his skin falling off him. His murderer is still out there. Still at large. Maybe standing behind this door waiting for us with a giant knife.

Okay enough of that.

Devon now bangs on the door.

"I think if he hasn't heard by now, that's not going to change anything," I say.

"This is weird."

"I say we take off. I don't like this."

"Let me check in the back."

"No, I wouldn't."

"Why?"

I hold Devon's arm for a minute. "Seriously—what do you think you'll find back there?"

"I don't know. Maybe a light or something. He could be in his basement completely bombed. Or listening to head-phones. You know."

"I'll go with you."

"No, stay here in case someone answers the door."

With a knife and a smile and blood on his hands . . .

"Wonderful," I say.

I hear his feet shuffling on the grass and around the side of the house. I look at the uncut lawn. They could use my ser-vices big time. Maybe I'll leave them a flyer. Of course, I have to make a flyer first. And yeah, I'm not going to be leaving anything here, not at this haunted little house.

I see something dark moving slowly across the lawn. Some kind of animal. Then I see a few more.

Cats.

I'm not a huge cat fan. Never have been. And the fact that these are just slinking around through the thick grass by this empty house . . .

"Devon," I call out, ready to get out of here.

I look at the door again, try to hear any kind of movement or sound.

Suddenly I hear Devon racing back toward me.

He's cursing in a high-pitched voice.

Instead of running to the front of the house, he darts through the yard and sends the cats scampering away.

"Devon," I rasp out in a loud whisper.

He opens the door of his Jeep. I think that's a sign for me to leave. Now.

I bolt back to his vehicle and tear open the door, biffing my arm in the process of climbing in. The Jeep is already started, and he shifts into drive and peels out.

We move about five feet before feeling a slight bump and hearing an animal scream.

A cat.

"What was that?" Devon asks, stopping. "What'd I just drive over?"

"Let's go."

"Get out and check," he howls at me.

"You get out and check," I tell him.

I don't even know what I'm doing here in the first place. This doesn't feel like I'm doing something for Marvel. This feels like I'm just being stupid and am going to wind up dead.

Devon gets out of the Jeep and looks at the front tire on the driver's side, then walks around to the front one on my side. I see him jerk back and wince and make a revolted sort of face.

He quickly climbs back inside.

"What was it?" I ask.

"We just killed a cat." He curses.

I can still see several others on the lawn. Watching. As if they're judging.

Hit-and-run, mister. We're calling the cops.

Devon turns around and speeds down the road.

"What'd you see behind the house?" I ask again.

He just shakes his head.

"What? Come on."

"I don't know."

"You like, freaked out and tore off after the car," I say. "You must have seen *something*."

"I don't know what I saw."

"What do you mean you don't know? Then why'd you act like you saw a ghost or something?"

"Well, I . . . I sorta did."

Devon shakes his head and looks at me. We're heading back to the main street in Appleton.

"What do you mean?"

He's breathing fast, and I know he's not goofing around.

"I went around and stood on the back patio. And as soon as I stepped on it, candles lit up all around me."

"Maybe a security system or something."

"I thought someone saw me and turned them on," he says. "But then I saw—I don't know what they were."

"They?"

"I saw these little things—white, glowing things—dancing in the backyard."

This makes me laugh. "What are you talking about?"

"I saw them. They were real."

"Glowing, dancing midgets?"

Devon curses. He doesn't find it amusing.

"Seriously?" I ask him. "Come on."

"I'm serious. Brandon, I swear. On my life. I'll swear on

anything. It's like—they were some kind of being. Spirits or something."

"Someone's totally messing with you."

Devon curses again. I can tell he's scared.

"No, they were real."

"How do you know?"

"'Cause I could just—I just felt something. Something awful."

I can't help it; I laugh. A nervous, freaked-out sort of laugh.

"They wanted us to go there, and then they don't answer the door," I say. "Then you go to the back and find glowing ghouls. Come on."

"I know what I saw," he repeats.

"Well, good news is we left them a dead cat too," I say.

Devon's not laughing.

We drive in silence for a few moments. I still don't fully believe him, but then again I do. I don't know what to think.

"You don't know what I saw," Devon says. "Or what I felt. It's real. Very real."

"I still don't know whether I believe you."

"You think I'm making that up? Go back there and you'll see it."

"No thanks."

We're at a stoplight and Devon turns to me, looking all strange and serious in spite of that mushroom of hair.

"What if that house is haunted or something?"

"Shut up," I say.

"I'm serious."

"Did you see anything else? Maybe an old dude playing with some lights."

"It smelled funny," he adds.

I laugh again.

"Fine, whatever," Devon says.

"Well, if you're so worried, maybe we should call the cops."

"And tell them what? They'll ask what we were doing there. No way."

When we get to his house and he shuts off the car, we remain in the Jeep for a moment.

"Devon, seriously, did you see that?"

He yells a curse at me. "Yes!"

"Okay, okay, I'm just asking."

"Why would I make that story up?" he asks. "I know how lame it sounds."

"I don't know."

"We can't tell anybody."

"I was thinking of telling my mom later tonight."

"Nobody. Not even Frankie or Barton."

"Yeah, could you imagine Barton hearing that?" I ask. "He'd go back there just to take pictures and post it on his Instagram account."

Devon doesn't laugh.

"Did you get another text from the guy you were supposed to meet?"

He checks his phone. "No. Maybe I will later."

"Let me know if you do."

"Nobody can know about this," Devon says.

"Yeah, okay," I say, then add, "not sure what I'd tell them. Mysterious glowing dwarves. Yeah. Okay."

Nobody would believe me anyway.

I don't believe it myself.

17

The figure seems to glide through the night. I'm standing on the edge of the road watching. As it gets closer, I see that it's a guy on a bike. It's late and the night is thick with darkness, but now I can make out Seth Belcher. He's riding with no light on and no light-colored clothing. The hood on top of his head only makes him blend in even more.

He's maybe twenty yards from me when a car's headlights come into view. It's racing down the street and accelerates the closer it gets to Seth.

Seth passes me, and a few seconds later the sports car passes. Then I see something coming from the passenger side of the car. Seth topples over, as if something was thrown at him.

I run across the street and find Seth crumpled up in the ditch. The side of his head is gushing blood, and he tries to hold it like some kind of water leak.

"What happened?" I ask.

"Greg," he says in a barely audible gasp. "Sergio. Think they threw a brick at me."

I hold him for a moment and start to scream out, searching my pockets for my phone. That's when I wake up.

I'm dragging this morning. It's the middle of the second week of school. I don't know if it's from soccer practice yesterday afternoon or from the nightmare I had last night. I half wish I was like Mom, who absolutely needs her coffee to start the day, but then I remember I don't like being overly wired. I'm eating some cereal when Dad stumbles into the kitchen.

He's looking rough. Like, really rough. Like I've seen him look on some really horrible occasions, ones that aren't nightmares but real-life terrors.

"Don't give me that look," he says.

I look away and don't answer him.

"You'll know one day, my boy," he says in a mean and sarcastic sort of way.

I have no idea what he's talking about. He opens the fridge and gets the orange-juice container.

"One day you'll know," he says, standing by the fridge.

I don't dare answer him. He's been drinking. I don't know if he's already been drinking this morning, but I know he's still full from the night before.

Mom has already gone to work. She thinks Dad is clean and sober. But he's neither.

"You grow up and there's ten thousand pressures you'll never understand now. *Never*."

He's standing there in jeans and a T-shirt, and he doesn't look as muscular as he used to. He actually looks a little thin.

I find this odd since he's supposedly *more* healthy now that he's "not drinking." He's holding the carton of orange juice while he glares at me. I can imagine him passing out, or throwing the carton of OJ at my head. I can imagine anything happening, which is awful. When you can imagine anything happening, then you do. Every single time you see the monster who is your father.

"It only gets worse," Dad tells me. "You'll see. You'll understand."

With this bit of advice, he takes the carton of orange juice and disappears into the other room.

When I get to school, my day goes from not so great to really terrible in a matter of seconds.

"Long time, stranger," says a voice at my locker.

I don't need to look to see who's talking. I close my locker and contemplate sprinting down the hallway.

"What's up?" Taryn asks.

She's looking extra animated and extra spicy today in her tight jeans and long-sleeved white T-shirt.

"Just going to class," I say.

"I know you can talk to me. That you don't have a *girl-friend* who will disapprove."

I wonder what she's talking about.

"Oh, don't give me that look," she says. "You know what I'm talking about."

"So you want to talk?" I ask.

"Of course. I miss you."

She tilts her head and looks all shy and innocent. This is how she gets everything in her life. I think she must've learned this when she was two years old.

"What do you really want, Taryn?" I say in my most cynical, skeptical voice.

"Ouch, that hurts."

"I'm just being honest."

"I miss our conversations."

"More like our arguments," I say as I start to walk to class.

"They weren't *all* arguments."

"Most of them were."

"Do you like that girl?"

Something in the way she says *that girl* doesn't seem very kind.

"Her name is Marvel."

"You do, don't you?"

I stop for a moment and look at her. "Why are we even having this conversation?"

"What?"

"I don't want to be mean or anything, but . . ."

"But what?" she asks.

It's like she's trying to get into an argument just to show that she can still get under my skin. And she can. This girl drives me crazy. In a bad way.

"Look, I'm just having a bad morning."

I never did tell Taryn about my father. She's too self-absorbed to have ever wondered or asked, either. I'm glad. I don't want people knowing my business.

"You going to the big party this weekend?"

I laugh. "Oh, yeah, totally. I was the first person they invited."

"I'll invite you if you don't know about it."

She tells me about the party at Ryan Jenkins's house Saturday night, but I don't care. I think someone mentioned it to me. Maybe Frankie. But I'm only interested in seeing Marvel. And I'm pretty sure Marvel isn't going.

"I can't wait," I say.

"Somebody's Mr. Grumpy," Taryn says, brushing back her hair and then stretching.

She keeps doing things that used to make my head twirl. It's just Taryn. Sexy Taryn. Really overdoing it this morning for some reason.

"That's me. Gotta go to class."

"Bye," she says with a full smile.

I'm not sure what she ate for breakfast, but I hope she doesn't start having it often.

18

It's Friday and I don't want to be around the guys and I don't want to do anything unless it's with Marvel. So at the end of the day I tell her exactly that.

"Let's hang out tonight."

"No."

She doesn't even hesitate.

"We don't have to do some kind of date thing or even anything fun."

"Then what are you talking about?" Marvel asks.

"I just want to be with you."

And I don't want you being alone with any crazy thoughts and images and nightmares.

"I don't know."

"Please, Marvel. Please."

"Why?" She pauses. "Why, Brandon? Why do you keep this up?"

"Keep what up?"

"Keep—keep asking me to do things. Keep trying to be around me. I've told you."

"I just want to be your friend."

She laughs in a cynical sort of way. This is when I know she really, truly is down.

"I do," I say.

"I won't be any fun tonight."

"That's okay."

I just don't want you to wallow in whatever your mood might be.

She's quiet.

"Anything," I say. "Seriously. Anything."

"I want to do something I've never done."

I think for a minute. "Like, skydive or something?"

"Nothing where I can die." She laughs at her own comment.

"Okay."

"Surprise me. You have an hour."

What?

"But I have to be surprised. If I'm not, I'm leaving."

This is new territory. This whole surprising-a-girl thing. Or really chasing a girl, one who doesn't even want to date, one who surely doesn't want to mess around. Which is fine, because I just want to be around her. She makes me feel better. And maybe, in some way, I do the same for her.

I have a few ideas, but all of them are suddenly destroyed the moment I get home and Mom says, "We need to visit Cousin Earl."

"I can't."

"You told me you'd go with me this week. Remember that

conversation we had? You said specifically, 'Sure, *Mom*, I'll go with you.' You know Earl likes seeing you."

Earl likes seeing any human being who can talk and move and smile.

"Mom, seriously, can you take Carter or Alex?"

"Brandon Edward Jeffrey—you are coming with me."

Things are not good when my mother uses my middle name.

"Come on—we're leaving in five minutes."

I sigh and look at my cell phone. I'm about to text Marvel that we need to cancel when a text from her appears.

So what kind of creative thing do you have in store for me tonight?

I stare at the text for a while, then I can't help but smile.

Oh, Earl is very creative.

Just you wait.

My mom calls Earl her cousin, but really that's not correct. Earl is the cousin of my mother's mother, who died of cancer when I was ten. He's in an old folks' home and suffers from dementia. Not Alzheimer's, Mom says— I guess Alzheimer's is a form of dementia, but Earl doesn't have that. He's just got a mind that seems to forget a lot and remembers odd details at the same time. Sometimes he has no idea who my mother is and other times he knows her well.

The place—"assisted living" is the term they use—is nice, but it still smells like old people. Old people and burned toast. I've gone there three times with Mom, and every time it smelled like someone burned toast in the kitchen. But it's nice, with a comfortable lobby to hang out in and nice rooms with flat-screen televisions and even a large dining room where everybody gathers for their daily meals.

I don't tell Marvel where we're going when we pick her up, and I tell Mom not to say anything. Mom makes small talk with Marvel, who doesn't seem at all surprised that my mother is driving us to wherever we're going. I keep turning around and looking at her in the backseat. The smile on her face says she's intrigued.

When we pull into our destination, Marvel reads the sign.

"Retirement village?" she asks me.

"Yes. I'm looking for places, you know. It never hurts to start early."

She laughs, but now she has a look of *what-in-the-world-are-we-doing?* I'm glad I have her full attention.

"So who are we going to see?" she asks me.

My mother is checking in at the front desk. Several older people, a couple in wheelchairs, are sitting in the lobby area. The television is tuned to a *Dateline* special about a man who murdered his wife.

"My cousin Earl. Actually my grandmother's cousin. He's—he's interesting." I laugh.

"Interesting how?"

"He's not all there. He's losing his mind. Like, literally. Forgetting things. Has dementia."

"Oh, I'm sorry to hear that."

"He also occasionally bites."

Marvel looks like she believes me, so I laugh and tell her I'm only kidding.

"That's not nice."

"I'm sorry," I say, still chuckling.

Marvel looks classic tonight, with baggy black pants and boots, a white shirt with a slim tie, and a full-length thick brown sweater. She's got a wavy, funky black hat to match.

"By the way, love the outfit," I tell her.

She's used to me saying this.

"Know what look this is?" she asks.

"Um—seventies?"

She rolls her eyes. "No. What look from the seventies? Remind you of anything? A movie maybe?"

I shrug. "I don't know many seventies movies."

"Ever hear of *Annie Hall*?"

I shake my head. "No, but I have heard of *Annie*."

"Good. Tomorrow I'll wear my red wig."

I make a mental note to myself to look up that movie she's talking about. She inspires me to do that a lot.

Mom waves to us, and we follow her to Earl's room.

Earl is sitting in a recliner chair watching television when we enter his room. The first thing I notice is that he's forgotten to shave half of his face. One side is clean-shaven with wrinkles and spots. The other half is sprinkled with gray-and-white stubble. He sorta stopped around the midway mark. Even his chin and upper lip are half done. I look at Marvel and can't help bursting out laughing.

"Earl, you have a new visitor tonight," my mom says, giving me the look to shut up and stop chuckling. "This is Marvel."

It's love at first sight. Seriously. Earl is utterly transfixed. I might as well be a nurse waiting to check his blood pressure.

"Valeria . . ." Earl says, taking Marvel's hand as if he's about to propose.

"No, Earl, this is Marvel. She's a friend of Brandon."

I smile but he doesn't notice me. He doesn't say anything back to Mom. He's lost in his own world. I wonder if it's the dementia, but then I realize I probably acted a lot like this the first time Marvel stepped foot into my life. I don't blame the old guy.

"I've missed you, my señorita," Earl says in a voice with an accent.

Mom looks at Marvel and gives her an *I'm sorry* sort of look. But Marvel just shrugs.

"It's good to see you again," Marvel tells Earl, giving him a kiss on his cheek. The shaved one.

"I still think of our weekend together."

Once again I can't help but let out an audible laugh. Now I'm curious.

I know Earl was married and had a couple of children. His wife passed years ago and the kids moved on. It's strange to think of Earl knowing a "señorita" who looked like Marvel and having a weekend with her.

"One of the best weekends of my life," Earl says. "I still remember the hotel room. The blue room, as we called it. Where we never left. We just talked and talked. When we weren't doing other things."

"Okay, then," Mom says, trying to get Earl's attention. "I think we need to finish shaving you."

"I already shaved today."

"You left just a little on your face."

Mom finds an electric razor while Earl continues to stare at Marvel. But Marvel never seems uncomfortable. She responds to a few of his comments, but she remains as vague as possible.

"Sometimes I dream about those days. I feel so young again."

"Okay, Earl. I think they need to leave for a while so you and I can talk."

Mom gives me the *get-out-of-here* look. I'm not sure what it's like for people like Earl to be confused. Will he snap out of it and realize Marvel isn't Valeria? And if he does, will he freak out?

Maybe this is why Mom wants us to leave.

"You haven't changed a bit," Earl tells Marvel. "But then again, I knew you never would. You would stay young and bright and beautiful."

Marvel nods and then does something unexpected. She gives Earl a hug.

"You take care of yourself," she tells him.

"I'll try. But you know me."

"I'll just be a few minutes," Mom tells me.

I walk out with Marvel and laugh again. "We found your long-lost boyfriend."

"Well, you win," she says.

"What?"

"I told you to surprise me. And you surprised me."

I look at an elderly woman moving past us with a walker. We both greet her.

"Can I interest you in a drink?" I ask Marvel when we're alone again in the main lobby. "Here in the gray room?"

"The gray room?" she asks.

"Yeah. It's not blue, but—well, it's the best I can do."

19

We've found a love seat to sit on while we wait for my mom. And luckily, I've found us some dinner to munch on.

"These are the best graham crackers I've ever had," Marvel tells me as she works on her second one.

"I hope you brought a big appetite. Because there's *lots* more where that came from."

"A big graham cracker closet?"

"Absolutely. And hey—you haven't commented on the cranberry juice."

"Well, I haven't opened it yet."

"Please, allow me," I say.

It's one of those cups where you peel off the top to drink. I asked a woman at a counter if they had any food and this is what she gave me. I'm not sure if she knew I was talking about for me and my "date," but I didn't want to complain.

Marvel takes a sip from her plastic cup. "Ooh, it's very . . ."

"Very what?"

"Very, uh, cranberrylicious."

I laugh and sip mine. "Only the best."

"We could be at a four-star restaurant and it might not be as memorable."

I look at her for a minute. "Seriously?"

"Okay, well, it might be memorable. But seeing my old flame just tops my month so far."

For a while we talk about school. Then we talk about soccer, and that morphs into family stuff. The good news is that my mom still hasn't shown up.

"I'd prefer not to dwell on my family life," I say.

"Are things better?"

I shake my head. "My dad is still drinking. Mom doesn't know. But the good news is I haven't been hit on the head with a vodka bottle or crashed into a car while Dad's driving."

She doesn't say anything.

"That was a joke," I say.

"It wasn't particularly funny."

"I know."

"I don't want anything to happen to you."

I nod. "Yeah, well, same goes for me."

Marvel tightens her lips and thins her eyes. "You still don't believe me, do you? That I heard God's voice telling me I was going to do something. That I was going to die."

I put the remaining graham crackers back on the table, then shift so I can face her. "It's not that I don't believe you. It's just—I'm hoping that it's not the case. I mean—what if you heard wrong?"

"It was pretty clear, what I heard."

"What if God changes his mind? Or some kind of miracle happens? Or a knight in shining armor comes to save the day?"

"Well, then, I'll be happy. Guess I'll have to find a knight around here. Know of any?"

"Funny. Look, I want you to be happy," I tell Marvel. "Now. And for a long time to come."

"I'm happy now. Tomorrow and the day after that—those are out of my control. There's a verse in Matthew. It says to not worry about tomorrow, because tomorrow will bring its own worries. Today's trouble is enough for today."

"Do you feel troubled today?"

She shakes her head. "No. And that's a good thing. Thanks to these graham crackers."

"And cranberry juice."

"Yes." She holds up her juice cup. "We need a toast."

I hold up my cup.

"Has anyone in the history of the world ever toasted with these?" I ask. "I mean—it's a bit of a pain saying, 'Hold on, let me peel off the top.'"

"I'm sure someone somewhere has. Probably a hopeless romantic."

"Are you calling me a hopeless romantic?" I ask.

"Uh, no. I'm the one making this toast, right?"

I smile. "Yes, you are."

"A toast . . . I hope one day you find yourself elderly and half-shaven and still able to remember sharing graham crackers and juice in the blue room—I mean the gray room—with your señorita."

"Cheers," I say.

"Cheers."

We drink our cranberry juice like shot glasses. Then I think of everything she said and can't help but let my smile fade a bit.

"What is it?" Marvel asks.

"I want to do anything possible—anything I can—to protect you. To save you. From whatever might be coming your way."

Those dark eyes look at me and almost force me to look away. Sometimes they're still too much. I feel so exposed when she looks at me that way.

"What if your job isn't to save me?" she asks. "What if it's to comfort me and feed me crackers and juice?"

"I can do both."

She laughs.

"What?" I ask.

"I guess if you can work for free for a whole summer just to talk to me, then . . . well, yes, Brandon Jeffrey. Maybe you can do both. We shall see."

"I say cheers to that," I say, lifting my empty cup. "That's a good thought to end the night on."

"Oh, no. This is all very nice, but I sort of expected this date to include dinner. Something more filling than crackers and juice."

"Like what?"

She smiles. I can't read her mind just yet. But I'm trying.

I keep getting a little closer each time I'm around her.

20

Ice cream. That's her dinner solution.

It wouldn't have been my first choice, but like I said, I can't read Marvel's mind just yet.

"This was sweet."

"The night or the ice cream cone?" I say. "Yeah. The date of the century. Blew you away, didn't I?"

"I told you to surprise me. And you did."

I just laugh. I dropped Mom off, and we're now in downtown Appleton having ice cream at the Scoop. I'd stay here until four in the morning with Marvel if I could. Just talking about anything. It doesn't matter. Just to see her smile and watch those eyes light up and hear her laugh. It's purely selfish, my being here with her. It gives me a delirious feeling. The feeling that anything is possible. The belief that I can—that I *will*—do anything.

Yes. Pretty wonderful.

"What are you thinking? I can tell your mind is running."

"I know," I joke. "It starts to smoke when it does that, right?"

She almost spits out ice cream she laughs so hard.

"Easy. It wasn't *that* funny."

"You know what I loved about tonight? Maybe almost as much as meeting Earl?"

"Let's see . . . the smell of the place."

"Stop," Marvel says. "No. I loved seeing you around the elderly people. Especially the woman we saw as we were leaving."

"Are you saying I'd make a great male nurse?"

"I'm saying that you have this big, seeing heart you carry around inside you."

I think about that as I continue to eat my ice cream cone. I know it's a compliment, but I have to really seriously think about the whole seeing part.

"What?" Marvel asks.

"I'm just picturing that big eye of Sauron from the Lord of the Rings movies."

"What?"

"Never saw them?" I ask. "They're amazing. Sorry."

"It's that you see things others don't. You're aware."

"Tell that to my brothers. They often say I don't even act like they're alive. And I probably don't."

"You make me *feel* I'm alive," she tells me.

"That's because all I think about is you. I mean—you know that, right?"

"I do."

"There's no reason we shouldn't be together," I tell her.

"Except, maybe, that God doesn't want us to be."

I stop eating my ice cream cone, I stop smiling, I stop joking around.

"What?" she asks.

But I don't say or move or do anything.

"Stop looking at me like that."

"What am I supposed to say to a comment like that?"

"I'm just being honest."

I nod. "Okay. So can I be honest?"

"I don't know."

But I make my own decision this time. "Why wouldn't a God above want us to be together? Even if—even if the things you say actually come true. Why can't I be with you? You said it yourself—how you feel when you're around me."

"Brandon—"

"I'm not giving up. I'm not. I mean—I brought you to an old folks' home. That's called determination."

"Or desperation?" Marvel says, clearly joking.

"Yeah, that too."

I reach over and touch her free hand. "I don't know what God has planned for you or for me or for whatever. I mean— I wasn't even really thinking about God until you came around. I still don't get all the things about him, but that's okay."

"You're right, it's okay," she says.

"And you and I are okay too." I grip her hand tightly. "We are. We can be together. We belong together, Marvel."

She closes her eyes and shakes her head.

"I don't understand why we don't. I can't."

"God told me we don't," she says, her voice barely managing to utter the words.

"You literally heard that? Or he showed you a picture of me with the word *No* scrawled over it?"

She nods and looks at me. "I know you think I'm crazy."

"I do. Completely. But you're amazing. No, I know you're not crazy, so the whole God-talking-to-you thing is just really—"

"Weird?"

"Endearing."

This makes her really laugh. Like laugh so hard I see tears in her eyes.

"What'd I say?"

"Nothing," she tells me.

"What?"

But she doesn't tell me. She just keeps laughing and wiping the tears from her eyes and then finishes her cone.

These girls—all of them—are such mysteries.

I don't want to take her home. I want to take her to our home, to our life, to our love.

As I drive slowly down the road, with the music she chose on the radio playing in the background, I think about what I'm going to say. What I'm going to do. I don't want tonight to end. I get a little dose of this girl and then I don't want to stop taking it.

You just compared her to medicine.

But maybe that's right. 'Cause she does make me feel better.

I arrive at the apartments and drive up to the curb. Then I shut off the car.

"Marvel, look—"

"Don't," she says.

"Don't what?"

"Don't talk. We've talked enough tonight."

She studies me the way a blind person might look at someone for the first time after being able to see. I feel weird, naked. Then she reaches a hand over toward my face.

She takes her other hand, and with both of them cupping my face, she slowly rubs the sides of my face. My jaw, my neck, then back up again.

"What are you doing?" I ask.

"I'm memorizing this," she says.

"Okay, but, um, isn't that something a blind person might do?"

"We're all blind in certain ways, aren't we?"

"I don't think I know what—"

Her finger slips over my lips, interrupting my words. It gently stays for a moment.

"You. Brandon. This beautiful soul. You make me feel something wonderful, you know that?"

Then the finger goes away, so I think I'm allowed to speak. "And what is that?"

"You make me feel like I belong."

"You do. You belong anywhere you want to be. You should know that."

"But I don't."

"Let me make you believe that," I tell her. I take her hands in mine. "Please, Marvel."

"You have such a tender soul."

"While I'm beating up people on the soccer field."

"You have a tender soul," she repeats.

"Okay."

"I haven't seen many guys who are that way."

"I'm sorry I'm the first."

She shakes her head and smiles. Her eyes light up, so alive.

"I'm not," she says.

And then she moves over and kisses my cheek.

Suddenly I can't move. I can't speak. I am set in stone, but it's a glorious chiseled sort of stone.

"Thank you for surprising me, Brandon. Again and again. And again."

I barely manage to utter a good night before she's gone.

I'm so weak. I just want to sink back in the car seat and close my eyes and picture her kiss again and again. Oh, and again.

Her figure disappears into the night. I hate it, that this bright, brilliant creature has to disappear into the blackness.

I'll see you tomorrow. And the tomorrow after that. And the next one too.

As I drive away, my hand touches my cheek where she kissed me. I know I'm completely into this girl, but wow. That's all I can say. Wow. And then some.

God, can we talk? Because seriously I need to strike some kind of bargain with you if you're really up there.

So sometime? Anytime?

Just let me know.

I'm here.

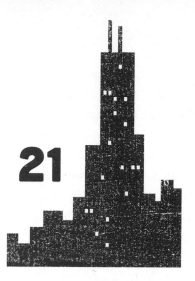

21

It's Saturday and I'm working five hours at Fascination Street. I had hoped that Harry would surprise me and tell me he scheduled Marvel today just like last weekend, but no such luck. Still, I'm glad to make a little money.

"How's the Honda working out for you?" Harry asks me in the middle of the day.

"It's great. I still owe you big time for it."

"Nope. It's a gift. Even if this store goes out of business." Harry laughs, but I can tell he's serious.

"You think it will?"

He nods. "Yeah. It's just a matter of time. Sarah and I are trying to figure out what's next. Maybe she'll go back to work and I'll be a stay-at-home dad. Or maybe I'll work on that novel I've always wanted to write."

"About what?"

"About a fortysomething following his dreams but broke and trying to support his family. Oh, and he's losing his mind."

"Do you want people to buy this book?" I ask, sorta joking but not really.

He lets out a big laugh. "Yeah, awful premise, right?"

"A bit depressing."

"Yeah. I need something better than that."

"What if a guy like you suddenly wins the lottery?"

Harry nods. "Then I start a band and we tour. Then my whole life goes down the drain when I lose my mind."

"I thought you'd already lost your mind."

Harry shrugs. "Yeah, maybe. My wife puts up with allowing me to dream. This whole store—it was a big dream, you know. But things don't always turn out the way they do in our dreams. Life happens. Things change."

I don't know what to say. I don't have dreams. Well, I have weird ones, but I don't have any long-range goals and passions. Unless Marvel is in them.

Harry asks me about her. It's something he does every time we're together now. I don't mind.

"We hung out last night."

"Really?"

"We're just friends," I say.

He groans. "Worst line ever. Seriously?"

"Not my fault. But it's complicated."

"We need to find something to remedy that," Harry says, heading for the turntable.

There's a musical remedy for anything in life, according to the curly-haired music geek.

"You're an album away from being rescued," I say, quoting one of the lines he uses a lot.

"So very true."

He puts on something that at first sounds like techno disco. I think I've heard it on a television show or a movie.

"Ever heard of these guys? Human League?"

I shake my head. "No. I might have to buy the album."

Harry knows I'm joking, since I never buy anything. "Make it vinyl. I have the original album here. It's called *Dare*."

The singer asks, "Don't you want me, baby?"

"Should I play this for Marvel?"

"You know—in my day we would make mix tapes."

I nod. "I've seen those . . . on the History Channel."

"Ooh, low blow, Brandon. My sons would love you."

We talk and joke. It's not like there are any customers to wait on. People who want music just go online and get it. Find it, borrow it, steal it. I don't know what it's called except reality. But it's fun to be in this place and try to believe that there still is some kind of business in the music industry.

"You know what I think women ultimately want?"

I shrug. The peppy, poppy sounds of Human League are still blasting through the speakers.

"Security. Think about it—when God created Adam, the two of them set everything up. Eve came along and found everything to be in perfect working order. Everything was *secure*. Of course, then she went and messed everything up."

"Isn't it the devil who did that?" I asked.

"Trying being married. There'll be days when Eve and the snake are one and the same." He laughs. "And don't you *dare* ever quote me on that. I'll get divorced and put in jail."

"Why do you say women want security?" I ask.

I'm trying to relate this to Marvel.

"I think guys look at a girl and think, *Wow, she's hot, she's awesome, I want her*. But females don't do that. Sometimes, sure, but it's more like, *Who is this guy and what will my world look like if I'm with him?*"

It seems to make sense.

"Look, I'm just saying—if Sarah had to choose between me and a seventy-five-year-old billionaire . . . well, I'm afraid to know the answer to that. I guess the motto is make a lot of money. Don't open a record store."

"You're telling this to a guy who worked the whole summer for free because he liked a girl."

Harry nods. "Yeah, we're both pretty hopeless, aren't we?"

The song playing goes, "Keep feeling fascination."

I wonder if it's an accident, but with Harry there's never any song playing by accident.

Which is sort of the way Marvel feels about God. That there's nothing that happens by chance or luck.

I'm guess I'm still on the sidelines, listening to the songs and watching the stories unfold.

22

I haven't spent a lot of time at Barton's house since last spring, when the moron crashed my car and then spent almost four months paying me back. Well, paying me back for the most part. He paid me in such little bits that it got confusing. I didn't want to create an Excel sheet to keep track; I just wanted my money. But we were finally all good and I've pretty much forgotten about everything. It still doesn't mean I fully trust the guy.

Or his family.

Frankie said he was going to Ryan's party, and Devon and Barton wanted to go too. So naturally I felt like I should, even though I didn't really want to see half the people there. Especially if Little Miss Popular with her blonde locks and swinging hips was going to be there. I asked Marvel if she wanted to go, but she only laughed.

Guess a laugh from a lady is enough to tell you her answer.

Turns out, the party starts back at Barton's house.

Barton's parents are . . . well, they're pretty laid-back when it comes to things like drinking in front of their children. Or letting their children drink in front of them. Or letting their kid's friends drink.

Yeah, didn't have to really wonder why Barton crashed my car. Not 'cause he was drinking, but because he was irresponsible.

So it's six in the evening, and Barton and Devon are both sipping on beer. Frankie's just hanging out. I refrain because the last person I want to be like is my father. Barton's parents are jamming the Bee Gees on the stereo and dancing in the kitchen, drinking whatever they have in their glasses. I'm thinking something harder than beer.

"I see your parents are into the seventies," I tell Barton above the noise of the music.

"Oh, yeah. They've always been a little that way. They're sorta leftover hippies." Barton looks around and then leans into us so we can hear him over the music and the television. "My dad still smokes some weed every now and then."

He gives Devon some kind of knowing look that makes me curious.

"He's smoked with me," Barton whispers, his round cheeks smiling with glee.

"Hey, Brandon, Marvel would love them," Devon says.

"Totally," I say, rolling my eyes.

Mrs. Menke comes in dancing and spilling her glass on the carpet. She doesn't notice, or maybe doesn't mind. They have a big chocolate lab that has already terrorized the carpet. They live in an older house with older furniture and things half falling apart—cracked blinds and lamps that don't work and an ancient, massive entertainment center with pieces always falling apart. They seem content to dance and party the night away, then do things like clean up after their big dog or replace the cracked blinds.

"Come on, get up, you lazy boys, it's time to dance."

From my place on a fake leather love seat I watch Barton and Devon get up, followed by Frankie. Soon all of them are singing the chorus of the Bee Gees song to me: "You should be dancing, yeah."

No, I think I should be back at the old folks' home, eating graham crackers with Marvel.

"Come on," Mrs. Menke says, grabbing my hand.

I think the party started for her a little while earlier today.

There are things I can do pretty well. I'm really fast, faster than most guys I encounter. I'm pretty good at soccer because of that fact. But I'm not good at moving and shuffling my feet around, and this means I'm not a very good dancer.

I give it my best for a few minutes, and the guys laugh at me. Especially Frankie. He changes the chorus: "You should be sitting down," he sings.

"I know. I got no soul."

He laughs. "You really don't."

Mr. Menke, who is short and chubby just like Barton, is watching us from the island in the kitchen, bobbing up and down. He's got a lot more soul than I do.

I wonder if this is what I have to look forward to when I grow up. Listening to forty-year-old songs and dancing and partying and forgetting about the dog they let out of the house about an hour ago.

"You guys ever see *Saturday Night Fever*?" Barton asks.

Devon has, but Frankie and I haven't.

"It's awesome. I want to be John Travolta's character for Halloween."

Barton looks nothing like John Travolta. But hey—he can try. He can dress up in seventies clothing and then he'll match Marvel.

Once the dancing is done Mrs. Menke leaves to refill her drink, since half of it slipped out onto the floor. Devon asks me if I told the guys what we found at the house the other night. I shake my head and give him a look to shut up. I think the two beers he's had are making him feel extra special tonight.

"What happened?" Barton asks. "This when you guys tried to buy some more pot?"

"Yeah," I say. "It's nothing."

"You should go to Colorado for that," Frankie adds.

"Totally," Devon says.

"So why didn't you get any?" Barton asks.

"Nobody was around."

Except, of course, some dancing, sparkling fairies. Or something like that.

"So what happened? Devon said it freaked him out."

I shake my head. "I think we need to get going."

"The party doesn't get started until nine," Barton says.

"Sorry. I'm not into that scene."

"Why don't you bring your girlfriend?"

I shake my head at Barton. "She's not my girlfriend."

"You two sure act like it."

"You know who's looking forward to seeing you tonight," Frankie says with extra ooh-ah in his voice.

"I know," I say. "I'm thinking of just taking off with her. Making it a long night."

"Shut up," Barton says.

He still can't believe how I *don't* like Taryn, even if it's just for an occasional night every now and then.

He doesn't know she's crazy.

"I'm only going 'cause you guys are."

"Party pooper," Barton says.

"Hey, some of us here are athletes."

"Really?" Frankie asks, standing up and looking around. "Did someone else get here I should know about?"

"Ha ha."

"Get kicked out of any games recently?" Barton asks.

"Extra ha ha."

"Do you think the Bee Gees talk like that in real life?" Devon asks. His mind is always wandering, especially with beer in him.

"Yeah, they sound *exactly* like that," I say.

"That's gotta be weird."

We all laugh. Devon can be so smart and then completely dumb at the same time.

I'm just glad we've moved off the whole strange house and magic lights on the back patio sort of thing. Nobody needs to know anything about that.

"You made it."

We're all at the party, surrounded by kids and music and laughter. And naturally, Taryn manages to find me two seconds after I step foot into the house.

There was a time when those words in that voice would have made me very happy. Like crazy happy. When I would have spent the rest of the night chasing after the girl speaking them. But that was back when I didn't know Taryn, when I didn't realize that all her little games were games. When she would play hard to get.

Now I'm the one playing that role, except for me, it's not an act. I'm totally over her.

"I'm not staying long," I say.

She's wearing an orange crop top and high-waisted jean shorts and a black cardigan that hangs over both. Chances are the cardigan's gonna get tossed later tonight.

"I don't see your little Latin lover."

Her voice is like fingernails on a chalkboard.

"She's waiting for me in the car," I say.

"You know—I like you a lot better when you're not chasing after me."

I laugh. That's funny because it's honest. Taryn's actually being honest.

Ryan's parents are around somewhere. They must be members of the same group Barton's parents belong to, the kind that are okay with kids drinking in front of them.

"You just can't stand someone *not* chasing after you," I tell her with a smile.

"We had some good times," she tells me.

Yeah, I remember.

Her eyes and expression say she'd like more of them.

"Didn't I see you and Ryan hanging around with each other this week?"

"Aww, that's so sweet," she tells me.

"What?"

"You noticed."

"We do go to the same high school, you know. We have some of the same classes."

"It's nice to know you're still keeping tabs on me," Taryn says. Then she sees someone else she wants to talk to. "I'll be back later."

The music is playing and the crowd is getting louder and I'm looking for the guys when we hear gasps and screams coming from the back. A wave of bodies suddenly pounds into me, and there's more yelling and cursing.

Then I see Seth Belcher running through the crowd, knocking people over.

What's he doing here?

Then I see someone chasing after him.

It's Sergio. One of the meatheads on the football team, and one of the guys who was beating up Seth the first time I really saw him. Sergio is holding his nose and cursing through his hand, which is covered in blood.

Did Seth do that?

I actually laugh out loud while people are all buzzing with the commotion and wondering what happened. I move toward the front door.

Maybe I'll have to intervene again.

I'm actually happy to do so.

23

I'm outside for a few minutes listening to the mayhem and, finally, seeing Ryan's dad break up the fight and order the guys involved to go home.

"Seth can come with me," I say.

Soon his bike is in the back of the Honda Pilot and we're driving away from the party. No big loss.

"So what happened back there?" I ask.

"Sergio wanted to pick a fight with me. So I picked up a lamp and broke his nose with it."

Seth looks wilder than usual, with his Mohawk haircut still in place. He's got a defiant look on his face. It's almost confidence.

Guess if I'd smacked Sergio like that back there, I might have some confidence on my face too.

"You know he's going to try to kill you," I say. "Either him or one of the other football players."

"I'll be looking out for them."

"What were you doing at that party anyway?"

"I have some friends there. They can't stop me from coming. What were *you* doing there? Doesn't seem to be your scene either."

I nod. "Yeah, I know. Frankie is friends with those guys. You know—Frankie Davis."

"The high school quarterback. How could I *not* know him?"

Seth talks without emotion. Or is sarcasm an emotion?

"You met him that night we picked you up over the summer and brought you home."

"Oh, how could I forget? Seems like this is a theme in your life."

"At least I have my own vehicle now," I say. "But I get it. Those guys are jerks."

"You get it?" Seth asks. "That's funny."

I almost forgot how difficult it is trying to get to know this guy. Like trying to pet a little dog and having it continually snap at your hand.

"Hey, man, I'm on your side."

"Sure," Seth says.

I don't say anything for a moment, but then I remember something I really wanted to ask him.

"Remember the night we dropped you off at that house? Where you said a friend of yours lives?"

Seth doesn't answer.

"You know," I press. "He lives at the end of a road—small house, dead-end street—"

"Yeah, so what?"

It's no wonder Seth gets his face busted up every now and then. He's so friendly.

"Who lives there?"

"Who wants to know?"

"The principal of Appleton High. Who do you think? I'm asking."

"Why?"

"Who wants to know?" I mimic his deadpan voice.

"Funny."

"Serious."

He looks at me for a minute. "You don't strike me as someone who smokes."

"I don't."

"Did you go there to buy?"

"Is that why you went there?" I ask him.

He shakes his head. "No. I mean, I've smoked pot, yeah, but it's not my thing."

"But you're friends with the guy who lives in the house."

Seth nods. "Jeremy Simmons. He's a trip." He laughs.

"Why?"

"Oh, you just gotta know him. Imagine if Jesse Pinkman from *Breaking Bad* had a brother who was more messed up than he was."

"He's a total stoner dude?" I ask as I stop the car at a red light.

We're almost to Seth's house.

"No. No, he's into harder stuff. He's pretty intense. That's all I can say."

"So why do you hang out with him?"

Seth looks at me for a minute. "Why do you hang out with a black quarterback, a nerd, and a total crack-up?"

"They're my friends."

"Yeah, well, we all have interesting friends then, right?"

So far, I've gotten nothing out of Seth. He's as strange as he ever was. Plus, I don't know anything about the guy we were trying to buy drugs from.

Except I know a name now. Jeremy Simmons.

"I'm just asking."

"Lots of people are asking things since they've found dead kids around here."

Seth says this in such an impersonal tone. Like a guy checking the dead body in a morgue. Talking about it in a clinical fashion.

"You know, man—this is like the—actually, I don't know how many times I've tried helping out."

"I'm not asking for help," he says.

"Yeah, okay. I'm getting the message. But you don't have to give me attitude."

We don't say anything else until I pull into his driveway. I help him get the bike out of the back. Then I remember my dream from the other night. Or the nightmare.

What if I hadn't been there to bring Seth home?

"Thanks for the ride."

"Yeah."

As I open my car door, he calls out my name. "Look— Jeremy and me—we've got some of the same tastes. That's all."

"Okay."

"I'll introduce you to him if you want me to," Seth says.

I nod. I'm not really sure if I want that.

"Cool," is all I say before telling him good-bye.

I think again about my dream and wonder where that came from.

When I'm home, I text Marvel.

Having a fun night?

I don't have to wait long for a reply.

No. I actually did some homework tonight. Can you believe that?

I tell her a few things about the party.

Sounds like I missed a great time.

Thought you said you were busy.

I know. I can see she's still writing something. **I've had some thoughts. On things.**

What things?

On you and me.

Oh no, I type.

No. These are good thoughts.

Really?

Yeah.

Care to share?

I will soon, Marvel writes. **Very soon.**

You promise?

Yes. I don't want to waste any more time.

24

I haven't been to church since I went with Marvel over the summer. For some reason, she hasn't invited me back. I think her uncle has something to do with it.

So on this boring Sunday, after spending the morning watching ESPN and an action movie with my brothers, I'm off to Portillo's to get us some lunch. Carter decides to come along to make sure I get his onion rings.

On the way he asks me an out-of-the-blue question. "Why didn't you play football?"

"I went for soccer instead," I say. "I was playing that before football was an option."

"I've been playing football since I was young."

I laugh. "You were born with a football in your hand."

"You sound like Mom."

"Yeah, I was quoting her."

"You could've played. You're fast."

"Why so interested?"

He shrugs. "Just wondering."

I don't want to tell him the truth.

It's 'cause our Dad sucks. And his whole life centers around drinking and football.

"I don't like the jerks who play football," I say, making up an excuse.

Which is true. I'm thinking of Greg Packard.

"Promise me something," I tell Carter, whose messed-up hair makes him look like he could be in a boy band. "Don't ever become a jerk. Be like Frankie."

"Yeah, he's cool."

"Totally."

I'm glad that my brother acknowledges that Frankie is cool. Some of the morons he plays with are not. But that's okay. There are lots of morons in this world.

Some decide to have children. Some have three boys. But that doesn't change them.

"Don't be a moron," I say to Carter.

"Like you?"

I punch him in the arm like I always do. Not hard. And even if I did punch him hard, he could take it. He punches back, and I yell out loud.

"Man, that killed," I say.

"Wimpy soccer player."

Marvel agrees to meet me later in the afternoon at Maxwell Park. I ask her if she wants me to pick her up but she says she's riding her bike there, so I decide to do the same. When I see her waiting on a small hill on the grass, I'm reminded of July 4 and the two of us sitting and watching the fireworks, not too far from where we are now. Then, for some reason, I'm reminded of her uncle threatening me. I wonder how far away he is at the moment and when he's going to pop up again out of the blue.

I've done what he wanted. I haven't been around their home. And Carlos hasn't seen me.

Not that you know of, anyway.

I focus on July 4, a more pleasant memory. I remember holding her hand. Her *allowing* me to hold her hand and her holding mine back. That was the night I told myself I wasn't going to let her go. That I'd be by her side whatever happened. Even if the sky fell, I'd stay right there.

And I'm still here.

"Nice day for a bike ride," she says.

"Yeah. Longer ride for you though." I sit down next to her. "What's up?"

"Just enjoying some fresh air. Our apartment gets a bit—cramped."

"I could be living in a mansion and it'd be cramped with my family."

"Everything okay?" she asks.

"Yeah. How about you?"

She shrugs. I don't push.

I look at her colorful blue T-shirt and jean shorts. Even when she's not being all seventies glam girl she still looks cool.

"I was thinking of something," she says.

"Let me guess. You wanted a graham cracker."

She laughs. "Absolutely. You know, I'm going to start calling you Graham."

"Okay, I'll call you Cranberry."

"No, just Berry."

"I don't know," I say, leaning in toward her a bit. "I think Cran sounds better."

"Sounds like Gran. And that sounds too much like Graham."

"Okay, you win. You're Berry."

"Good."

"Okay, well, nice chatting with you then . . ."

"Stop," she says, pulling back her wavy hair. "I was wondering about homecoming. It's next week."

"Ah, that's right. You know I'm going to be homecoming king, right?"

"I didn't see your name as a finalist," Marvel says.

"Wait, I'm not? Come on."

"Frankie is."

"Yeah. That jerk."

"Do you want to be on the homecoming court?"

I shake my head. "I've never given it a thought, to be honest. There's a pep rally, and the school gets all jazzed about alumni coming back and all that. Then there's a game—oh, wait, it's football, so who cares."

"You're forgetting something."

I see her bright eyes and even brighter smile. I'd ride a hundred miles to see them. Any day of the year. Any time.

"Oh, how Taryn might actually be homecoming queen?"

"No, that's not what I'm talking about. The dance."

"Ahhh."

Now I know why she's talking about this.

"Oh, I see. You're worried, right?" I say. "You need a date."

"I've actually been asked, thank you very much."

"Seriously?"

"Yes, seriously." She mocks being offended. "There are some guys interested in me."

"Of course there are. Who asked you?"

"That's not my point."

"But come on. Who?"

She looks like she's not going to tell me. "Okay, fine. Well, one of them was Greg. Your lovable Greg Packard."

"Are you serious?"

She nods.

"Oh, and when were you going to tell me this?"

She shrugs, acting all innocent and flirty.

"I'm not *even* going to ask what you said, because I already know."

"Oh you do, huh, Graham?"

"Yes I do, *Berry*."

"I think I sorta laughed in his face."

I give her a high five. "You are my new hero."

"I did tell Mitch yes, however."

"What?"

"I'm joking," she says.

"So, your 'thoughts'—they're about the homecoming dance?"

Marvel shakes her head. "No. What I said the other night . . . what I texted . . . No. I was just wondering—if you actually go to homecoming. You know, being a soccer player and all."

"I know," I say. "Us soccer outcasts. Of course I do. You'll go with me, right?"

"Is that you officially asking?"

"Do I need to do something to make it official? Buy you a corsage or something?"

She pushes at me. "No. But that's what I get? 'Uh, yeah, so you'll uh go with me, right, duh?'"

"I don't sound like Frankenstein, thanks a lot."

She doesn't reply. I clear my throat and turn to face her. Then I take her hand.

"My dearest lady, my lovely summer señorita. I wonder if you have it in your heart to do me the greatest honor and accompany me to our homecoming dance?"

She nods, then leans over and kisses my hand. "Yes, I will."

"Ooh, a kiss," I say. "I'm never washing that hand again as long as I live."

25

It's late Monday morning at school when Devon shows me the text.

Next time come alone.

"When'd you get this?" I ask.

"Last night."

I don't have to ask who it's from. The question is, why should it matter that I went with Devon to go buy pot? They're legalizing it in some states, so why is it that big of a deal?

Unless there's something bigger going on . . . which is, after all, why I went.

"Maybe you just don't go at all next time," I say.

"No, I'm planning to."

"Did you reply?"

"Yeah."

"Did you ask him what the heck the light show was behind his house?" I ask.

"No."

"I'm serious, Devon—I'd stay away if I were you."

"Don't you think this is all a little odd?"

I nod. For a moment I think about telling him about the conversation I had with Seth, but then I decide not to. I don't want Devon bothering Seth. The poor guy already has enough people messing with his business. Maybe I can learn something about Seth's "friend" myself.

"People dying isn't just 'odd,'" I say.

"They still don't know anything about Artie Duncan's death. They're not reporting on it as much."

"Just because you don't hear about things in the news doesn't mean they're not still trying to figure out what happened," I tell him. "But remember—you're not a detective, no matter how many cop shows you've watched."

"I'm not trying to be anything."

He doesn't sound too convincing.

"This isn't a video game," I say.

He laughs. "And you're not my mom."

"Thank God."

Before I head into my classroom, I ask him something I still have no answer for.

"The things you saw behind the house," I say. "What do you think that's all about?"

"I don't know. But I know how I felt when I saw it. I felt like I was witnessing something evil. Something dark and awful."

The scary thing isn't what Devon says. It's that he leaves without saying anything more.

I'm closing my locker door when this girl suddenly shows up smiling.

I don't know her name. She's in a couple of my classes,

but everybody just calls her Reebok because that's all she wears. Like *always*. Today she's wearing a blue Reebok sweatshirt, jeans, and Reebok tennis shoes. I suddenly remember that her name is Piper, but no one besides teachers ever calls her that.

"Hello, Brandon."

I smile and nod. "Uh, hi."

"Saw that fight of yours on the soccer field last week. Way to represent."

I shrug.

Piper is on all the sports teams. Basketball and track and probably other ones, too. I remember seeing her once on the track, and I couldn't believe how muscular and cut she was. She definitely could beat me up.

"I'm wondering if you'd like to go to homecoming with me."

I look around thinking—no, *knowing*—that Greg put her up to this. The resident football moron is just having some fun. I don't see anybody watching, but I just know.

"You want to go to homecoming? Like the dance?"

She laughs. She's actually quite pretty, which is something I've never noticed before.

"Yeah, that's what homecoming is. You know—the game, the dance, the court, dinner."

I'm still looking around to see if this is some kind of prank.

"You know—actually, I'm taking someone else."

And strangely enough, she asked me too.

I mean, I'm a total heartbreaker.

"Okay, that's cool. Are you—are you going with Taryn?"

"No," I say as if she asked if someone had died. "No, no, no. With Marvel. The new girl."

"Haven't talked to her. Dang. Okay. Well, maybe we can just grab dinner sometime. If that's cool."

"You want to go out to eat somewhere?"

"Yeah, that'd be cool. If you want to."

This is a total prank. It has to be.

"Yeah, definitely," I say, playing along.

They're not going to sucker me.

Reebok just smiles and then pats me on the back. I feel like I just got hit by a baseball bat. This girl is tough. Maybe a little too tough for me.

"Cool, maybe next month then?"

I still think she's just playing me. "Oh, yeah, sure thing."

"All right. Let's talk later."

She nudges me, and I slam into my locker.

Whoever set this up thinks they're funny.

I head to class. I can't wait to tell the guys about this. Oh, and Marvel too.

26

It's not like I'm scared. No. I think the term is creeped out. That's it.

It's close to midnight, and I know I need to be home since it's a weeknight. I told my Mom I was watching a movie at Devon's, which is true. It was a crazy horror movie, the over-the-top kind that Devon loves. In this one the next-door neighbors were Satan worshipers and did all sorts of weird things to the nice family beside them. At first it's kind of funny until they kill the sweet little dog and . . . well, let's just say it's very disturbing.

I know it's all make-believe and the blood and guts are typical gore. The thing I can't stop thinking about is that a group of people spent weeks or maybe months filming this. Making a whole crazy film about some dark, twisted people. Would they get their morning coffee and drive to work and laugh and joke and act like normal people before acting out the awful stuff on the screen?

"Well, that was pleasant," is all I manage to say at the end of the film.

"Need a ride home?" Devon jokes.

"No," I say. "But I'm never checking my mailbox again. Like ever."

The evening is cool and the sky is overcast, making it extra dark. But it never gets dark around here. Not like it does in the country. There are always lights on somewhere. It always feels like there's someone close by.

I'm halfway home when a car slows down and starts to follow me.

Not again.

The same thing happened a few times this summer. At least I don't think I was imagining things.

This time the car speeds up a little and then stops right next to me. It's an older truck, a Dodge Ram that's big and grumbles. I breathe a sigh of relief, because I know the owner before the head appears from the truck window. It's Phil, the old hippie who works at Fascination Street Records.

"What are you doin' out here on a weeknight?" he asks.

"I live just down the block," I tell him. "What are you doing?"

"Oh, I play cards with some buddies every Tuesday night. Well, more like I give them my money every Tuesday night. It's fun. Low stakes."

"Sounds like fun," I say.

"You want a ride?"

"It's okay."

"Aw, come on. It's late. If something happens to you tonight I'm going to feel really bad, you know?"

I guess he has a point. I circle around the intimidating vehicle and climb inside. It smells like tobacco in the cabin and the radio is playing seventies music. Phil reaches over to turn it down.

"Mom warned me about taking rides with strangers," I tell him.

"Good thing I'm not a stranger."

I laugh and nod. But suddenly, at midnight after watching a movie about satanic neighbors living next door, I can't help but be a little freaked out. Phil's always been a bit of an odd duck. I don't know if it's because he did too many drugs in the seventies or because he's still doing drugs. Though he tends to talk about Jesus a lot, which makes me think he doesn't do drugs. Or anything really strong.

"You working much these days?" I ask him as he drives slowly down the road.

The engine sounds louder than any I've heard. Maybe it's one of those super-jacked-up engines. Phil just grumbles.

"Nah. Not much. I'm at the record store more for fun than anything else."

"You think it's going to stay open much longer?"

"I think it's a miracle that store still exists," Phil says, then adds with a low laugh, "kinda like it's a miracle that I'm alive."

"Oh, yeah?"

He nods. "Where's your house?"

"I'm the fourth one on the left."

I figure if he was going to kill me, he'd be driving a lot faster.

"Yeah, I was a wild boy when I was your age. But those were different times. Although I have to say—evil is still evil. It's just we got a lot more of it these days. And it shows up in strange ways."

I nod. I assume he's talking about the two teens who were killed, but I'm not sure. With Phil, one never knows.

"You can just let me off here, thanks," I tell him.

"Hey, Brandon?"

I turn to look at him, and he shuts off the radio altogether.

"Do me a favor, okay?" he says.

"Yeah."

"No more walking around at night by yourself. You got that?"

I nod. "My friend's house is really close by."

"Yeah." He scratches at his scraggly white beard. "But it doesn't matter, 'cause evil's always close by as well. You understand?"

"Yeah, okay. Thanks."

I walk down my driveway and hear the rumbling engine heading on down the road.

Phil doesn't know that I understand only too well what he's talking about. As I stare at the dark windows of my house, I know evil is very close. Hopefully asleep by now.

27

I've been asleep for probably an hour when a text wakes me up.

I get out of bed and go to my desk to get my plugged-in phone. I squint my eyes and see Marvel's name.

Having a rough night.

I sit on the edge of my desk chair, where I never sit to do homework. I start typing and have to try several times to write what I want.

Why?

I know it's not very long, but I'm groggy.

I thought you'd be sleeping, she says.

What's wrong?

Thinking of my family. Really missing my sister. My mom. Have been crying for a long time.

I have no idea what to say. What can I possibly say or do to help in any way?

Wish I could cheer you up.

Knowing you're there does, she writes.

Well, that's good. I'm sorry, Marvel. I still can't believe everything you've gone through.

I wait for a while, but nothing comes. I don't want to pressure her. I've never wanted to push her to talk about her family.

Then she says, **I can't believe the evil in this world. It makes me sick. And scared too. I try to find comfort in Scripture. But some nights, like this one—it feels like God and heaven are so far away.**

I can relate to her last line.

But I'm not.

That's all I can say.

And I'm really glad, she writes back. **To imagine coming here and not having someone like you—I don't know what I'd do.**

You and Barton would be BFFs, I type.

I wish you could see me now, she writes. **I'm laughing while tears stream down my face.**

I want to tell her not to cry, to let me take her tears away from her, to let me take this sadness away. But I don't.

Barton makes everybody cry, I joke.

Sometimes I ache. Do you ever? Just ache because of feeling so bad?

I look at the question. I don't want to answer it. Really, I don't. I've gone this long without answering it. With taking the brunt of my father's misery. Just taking it and sucking it up and taking more.

Yeah, I say.

You're never far away, you know?

I could ride my bike to your apartment, I tell her. **Or drive.**

No, I mean, never too far away from my thoughts. It's like you're always in the passenger seat next to me while I drive through life. You know?

Can we stop through an Arby's? I write. Cause I'm hungry.

You're funny.

I try. Better than crying, you know?

Yes. Very much so.

I wish I had the words to say something now, something meaningful and poignant, something right. Something that will send her off into the dark night feeling a little lighter. But I have nothing.

Can you imagine a place where you don't have to ache? A place where the leaves turn red and orange and yellow every day. The place where you don't have to carry bags under your eyes or under your heart.

Sounds pretty cool to me, I say.

'Cause it does.

Do you know how I know God loves me? she writes.

I chuckle. Marvel and her talk about God. She makes him a little more real every time she mentions him.

I don't know, I text.

It's because he put you in my life. The feisty soccer player who won't give up.

I never knew I was so persistent, I tell her. Until meeting you.

It's a nice trait. Don't ever let that go, okay?

I won't.

Go to bed, Marvel writes. Again.

Okay. But text me if you want to. Okay? I'm here.

I know. I think I finally have got that in my head. And my heart.

This is a nice thing to wake up to and then fall asleep against. I don't know what else to say to her.

Nice to know, is all I write.

Yeah, I could do better. So I tell her, **A hundred other things I could say, you know?**

You already have without saying them!

Good night, I write.

So long, farewell, auf Wiedersehen, good night.

I'm not sure what that's all about but I won't ask. I've already gotten more than enough.

I don't think I'll be having nightmares tonight.

28

The team we're playing for our big Friday homecoming football game is tough, but in the fourth quarter we're up 34 to 20 with only a few minutes left. I'm only watching because of Frankie. Yeah, sure, it's my school, but I haven't really gotten into the weeklong spirit celebration. No, I didn't wear pajamas on Pajama Day. It's not like I'm trying to be rebellious or anything, but I'm just not into that scene. I've got other things on my mind. Like Marvel and making sure I avoid vodka bottles thrown by my father. But I'm cheering on the football team because of one of my best friends.

Frankie's really had a great game. He's thrown a couple of touchdowns and led the offense to two other rushing scores. He's not the most dazzling player ever, but he can manage to get out of the way of defenders and he throws the ball lightning fast.

The offense still has the ball and they're just running it to play out the game. I'm not paying close attention; I'm talking with Devon and Barton, who are sitting next to me in the stands. No Marvel tonight. It's a third-down play and Frankie takes the ball. Then something weird happens.

The offensive lineman in front of Frankie seems to just take the play off. He moves to one side and stands there while a couple of defenders rush over the quarterback. Frankie doesn't just get sacked. He gets sandwiched and squashed and almost snapped in half.

Everybody in the stands gasps, and then a hush like a wave covers the field. Frankie is lying crumpled on the grass field. A few of his teammates rush to his side, and a trainer and the coach head out to see him.

"Dude, he got annihilated," Barton says.

I'm searching for the offense lineman who didn't block the defenders . . . looking, looking, but I already know.

There he is. Standing off to the side. Not even going over to see if Frankie is hurt.

Greg Packard.

I curse as I look at the smug guy just standing there, doing and saying nothing.

"What?" Devon asks.

"That sack wasn't an accident," I say.

"What do you mean?"

"I mean Packard let him get crushed."

"Serious?" Barton asks.

"Totally. He just made sure they were ahead and couldn't lose."

"Why would he do that?" Devon says.

It has to be because of my sticking up for Seth, I tell them. The different run-ins that Greg has had with Seth. And with me. Then I share what I really think of the guy.

"Whoa, easy, killer," Barton says. "Brandon with the potty mouth."

We see Frankie pop up on the field, sitting now. The crowd applauds. Then Frankie is on his feet.

If the quarterback could have suddenly gained even more popularity after a resounding win, he just did.

He looks like he's okay, just woozy, and as he's helped off the field he waves to the crowd. We all cheer.

Greg is still standing there as if nothing happened. Everything inside of me wants to get back at this guy for being alive. For breathing air and thinking he's entitled to a little more of it than everybody else.

It turns out Frankie is fine, just got the wind knocked out of him. They did a hundred and one tests on him to see if he has a concussion, but he's okay. That means he can hang out with us afterward.

So Devon drives us back to his house, where we'll order a pizza. Now that nobody else is around, I ask Frankie about the hit.

"Did you see what happened?"

"Yeah. A couple of linebackers sat on my head."

"No," I say. "Did you see Packard?"

"What about him?"

"Brandon thinks he did it on purpose," Barton says.

"No, I don't 'think,'" I spit out. "I *know*. He let you get sacked, Frankie."

"What?"

"I'm serious. Do you guys film the game?"

"Yeah. Nothing elaborate, but the coaches want game film."

"You watch it," I tell him. "Greg literally just stepped to the side and let them come in. Then he stood there. Like the play was over. *Right* when you were getting mauled."

"Frankie, you think it was on purpose?" Devon asks.

"Maybe."

"What's he been like lately?" I ask. "A jerk?"

Frankie doesn't say anything, which isn't good. Normally he's the peacekeeper, the laid-back guy. But now he doesn't say anything.

"You think this has to do with the stuff this summer?"

Frankie looks back at me from the front seat. "Yeah."

Devon and Barton can't believe it.

"It's been building," Frankie says. "This must be retaliation for the party."

"But that was freako-kid Seth's fault. You didn't do anything."

Frankie nods at Devon's comment. "Yeah, but Brandon took him home."

"It's all *your* fault, Brandon," Barton says to me.

I punch his shoulder and tell him to shut up. "I'm just standing up to ignorant bullies."

"It's done," Frankie says. "We won the game and I'm just a little sore. No big deal."

I have an idea. "Hey, Frankie. Is there a party going on for the football players?"

"Yeah, for some. Of course."

Before we arrive at Devon's house, I ask the guys a question.

"Any of you want to play a prank? Maybe get back at the idiot who let Frankie get smushed tonight?"

"Oh no," Frankie says.

I spray some of the paint on the grass just to make sure the can is working. Then I leave the can on top of the hood of the Camaro. The sound of music and cheering can be heard from the huge house, but it's set way back from the curb and there's no way anyone inside can hear our muffled laughs.

"What's that for?"

We've already emptied several cans of temporary spray paint onto Greg's silver sports car. Well, it *used* to be silver. Now the hood flaunts a very bright pink flower. Which is the best image to represent this guy who sucks at life.

"That can is permanent paint," I say. "I want him to *really* freak out for a minute."

"Let's go," Devon says, looking toward the house.

We're in Glenforest Estates, close to where Taryn lives. Maybe I should've gotten some extra spray paint and done her car as well.

Sometimes I get a glimpse of what life would look like if I was still with Taryn. I'd be miserable, first off. But I'd also probably be here having to talk to a bunch of guys I don't know about a game I didn't play in. I'd also have to be at Taryn's side the whole time. Like some kind of bodyguard or butler.

No thanks.

"Come on," Frankie calls out after me.

We walk down the street and then turn to where Devon parked his car.

"This is crazy," Frankie says. "I just spray-painted the car of our best offensive lineman."

"Who purposely got you smeared all over the field tonight," I remind him.

"And whose dad is a cop," Frankie reminds me. "You better hope he doesn't find out. Seriously."

Barton and Devon can't stop laughing.

"I don't care if he does," I say as I climb into Devon's Jeep.

"No, Brandon—seriously. They can't find out I was a part of this. I'll lose the team."

"They won't."

"They'll probably just think it's Seth Belcher, and he'll end up getting beat up again."

I think about Devon's statement as I get into his car. He's probably right.

I didn't think of that. It's actually not a very comforting thought.

29

"Have you had any thoughts about college?"

Every now and then I think Mom has to scratch off *Talk to Brandon about college* on her to-do list.

"Absolutely," I say, then add, "not."

"Brandon."

"I know. I guess that's what people do after high school."

"You have to get serious about this."

I'm in my bedroom on my laptop and am not even looking at Mom, who stands in my doorway.

"Did you look at the websites of the schools I wrote down?"

"Not yet," I tell her.

My goal is to get far, far away from here. California or Arizona or Florida. But I guess my first goal should be to get serious with applying.

"Brandon?"

She's got a tone I have to turn for. It means she's waiting for me to look her in the face.

"I know you don't know what you want to do yet, but just tell me you can think about it every now and then."

"I will."

"No, I mean it. I don't want you sitting in this room five years from now, still trying to figure out what you want to do."

I laugh. "Don't worry. *That's* not going to happen."

"Well, you have to have a *job* to live on your own."

"Maybe I'll marry rich," I joke.

"That is one option," Mom says. Then she adds in a tone that I'm sure is joking: "That's what I used to think too."

Then she leaves. Maybe she wasn't joking.

That's the biggest warning I could get from her. 'Cause she dreamed big and then ended up . . . with Dad.

Yeah, maybe I do need to get a little serious.

A weird thing happens after my soccer game. It's not really a homecoming game like the football game was last night, but we still get more of a crowd than usual. We win 5 to 2, with me scoring a couple of goals. I've been playing better ever since that miserable game the other week where I got kicked out. Maybe that ignited something. I'm not sure.

At the end of the game, when I'm heading to the stands to say hi to Marvel, who's been smiling and waving at me, I hear someone call out my name. I turn to see Seth standing by the fence.

"Hey, man," I say.

"Good game," he tells me.

He's wearing a leather coat and a military-style cap. Both look too big on his tall but skinny frame.

"You watch the whole thing?" I ask.

"Yeah."

"Cool. Since when do you come to soccer games?"

He ignores my question. "I wanted to give you something."

"Yeah?"

"An address."

He hands me a business card. It's for Comcast, the guys we get our Internet and phone from. The name on the card is Jeremy Simmons. The guy with the house with the fairy lights.

"I'm seeing Jeremy tomorrow night. You got plans?"

"No."

"Come around ten o'clock."

"What is this? A house?"

Seth shakes his head. "No. It's a barn. An empty one."

"And what's going on there?"

"A party of sorts."

I look at the card, then back at Seth. For a second I check on Marvel, who is now standing and waiting by the stands.

"I know you have to go see your lady," Seth says.

"Yeah. But—like, what kind of party?"

"You wanted to meet Jeremy, right?"

I nod.

"Oh, and show up alone, okay?" Seth says.

Then he takes off toward the parking lot. I hold on to the card, not quite sure what to think about it.

Marvel greets me with a hug and a "Good game."

"I'm pretty gross to be hugged," I say.

"Never. So you got your two goals."

"Lucky shots," I say.

"You're good."

"Thanks for watching. I play better when my parents aren't around."

We walk toward the parking lot. I scan ahead for Seth, but he's gone.

"Who was that guy?"

"Seth Belcher," I tell her. "He invited me to a party tomorrow night."

"He goes to our school, right?"

I nod. "He's the one I told you about—the kid those football guys were messing around with."

"So you guys have become buddies?"

It's funny to hear how she says that. "Buddies? I don't know about that. He's an odd guy."

"Some people probably think I'm an odd girl."

"No, no. There's unique—that's you. Seth is just—he's just out there. Still haven't figured him out."

"But you're trying, right?"

I shrug, still holding the card he gave me. "I guess. I'm just excited that the game is over and I can take you on a real, true official date."

"Are you going like that?"

My white uniform has mud splattered all around it. My legs are muddy, too. The back of my shirt that was wet from sweat is now half dry.

"Yeah, you ready?" I joke.

"So five o'clock," she tells me. "Pick me up?"

I nod. "I can't wait."

"Me too."

Then Marvel gives me a look that I haven't seen from her yet. It's the kind of look that's not holding anything back. That's not hiding a single thing. And I really think it says that she's crazy about me.

30

I see her standing by her apartment building like some guardian angel in white. Or maybe some kind of princess waiting for her prince. Or maybe a grown fairy hiding her wings behind her white dress with the cut-out sleeves. I pull the car up beside her and then dash out so I can open her door.

"Wow."

That's all I can say to her.

"Like my outfit? I made it."

Her skirt hangs above her knees and is white and ruffled, just like those wild sleeves. She turns like some fashion model. The back has some kind of bright silver-and-gold pattern, and she's wearing these funky shoes that look like a combination of sandals and high heels.

As usual, I feel way too normal to be around Marvel. I'm wearing black pants—basically black jeans—along with a dress shirt, but I'm not even in the same league.

I say it again. "Wow."

Her smile is enough to make me temporarily forget about

her uncle. Or to really forget about anything bad and negative in my life.

When I get behind the wheel, I pause for a moment.

"So this is really an official date, right?"

Marvel nods, that sunshine smile still staring me down.

"Okay. Good. Well, Harry gave me this last time I was at the record store."

I open the CD case and take out a disc marked *Brandon and Marvel*.

"What's that?"

"Harry made us a playlist."

"Aww," she says. "He's so sweet."

"I know. He knows I need help. I only work at a record store. Doesn't mean I know music."

"Is this going to depress us?" Marvel jokes.

"I don't know. I haven't listened to it."

The first song begins to play, and it's a simple and soft guitar melody. When the woman starts to sing, Marvel makes that *aww* sound again.

"What?"

"Oh, come on."

"What?" I ask. "Who is it?"

"Stevie Nicks."

"Of course. Should've guessed it."

"I've never heard this version though."

We start to drive, and the chorus plays and I realize that Harry's pretty good at this playlist thing.

"Drove me through the mountains, through the crystal-clear water fountain, drove me like a magnet, to the sea, to the sea."

Marvel reaches over and takes my hand.

I wonder if she's changed her mind.

"This was a Fleetwood Mac song, but it's being sung by Stevie," she tells me.

I nod, but I don't really care. Stevie and Fleetwood and the rest of the Macs could all be in the backseat serenading us. I wouldn't care. All I care about is this girl holding my hand. This girl who finally found me.

It's crystal clear to me what I think, Marvel.

"You want to just drive around and listen to music and then end up in Key West?" I ask her.

She shakes her head. "No. Because we're meeting Devon and his *date* for dinner."

"Oh yeah."

I make a funny face. This nice mood will last only so long. Dinner is going to be . . . well, it'll be a first.

"You actually showed up," I say as I greet Devon a little more officially than normal. But that's because I'm talking to his date, Gina Broadfoot.

"I did," Gina cries out as if she's in a gym and not a steakhouse in downtown Geneva.

Gina gives me a big hug as if we've been friends our whole lives. I'm still not sure what color her hair really is since she dyes it all the time. I think it used to be red before it was blonde and orange and pink. Today it's blonde with streaks of blue.

"What's up, man?" I say to Devon.

This wasn't his idea, of course. He'd never decide to ask a

girl to an event, even if he liked her. This was something that happened last week when Gina came up to me and basically forced me to get Devon to go to homecoming with her.

Gina goes to the table to greet Marvel while I stay back for a moment with Devon.

"You still never said if you were actually going to go with her to the dance," I tell Devon with a laugh.

"That's 'cause I'm still deciding."

I crack up. We've known Gina since freshman year. She's an oddball who doesn't fit any mold. She's geeky but doesn't really hang out with that crowd. She's not truly an alternative girl, and she's definitely not a jock. Not that those categories necessarily apply—my group of friends, of instance, doesn't fit one type. But Devon and I just don't really know Gina, who seems to drift from crowd to crowd. She's friends with everybody. She's musical and she's definitely outspoken.

"Well, she's the one who came up to me and forced the issue," I tell him.

"She acts like she's had a case of Mountain Dew."

"Better than a case of beer. Right?"

We sit down at the table with the girls. It's so obvious we're the high schoolers going to the homecoming dance tonight, since we're surrounded by adults my parents' age and older. Some much, much older. I look at a menu and think it's crazy that we're here and not at Chili's. Almost thirty bucks for a steak? I'm thinking I'll get a salad and water.

"You used to live in Chicago? How cool is that? Do you get to go back there a lot? Don't you just love it?"

Gina is already asking Marvel a hundred questions.

Marvel, naturally, is so sweet while she talks to Gina. They couldn't look more different—Gina with her bright hair and her colorful outfit with strange tight pants and exotic shoes.

"Glad you picked a cheap place," I say to Devon.

"Glad you *got* me to come," he tells me in full sarcasm.

The girls don't hear us talking. Gina doesn't hear anybody, in fact. She just sort of talks and talks. Maybe that's why she doesn't seem to have one really close friend. Nobody can take *that* much talking and energy and wide eyes looking right into yours.

"I think the whole idea of a homecoming court is stupid, but I'm looking forward to watching it anyway and then taking this guy out on the dance floor."

I raise my eyebrows at Devon, and he just laughs. Gina needs a mute button, or at least a pause button to allow others to say something. Anything.

"I'm *so-o-o-o* glad you're not with Taryn anymore," Gina tells me. She looks at Devon and then at Marvel. "I know a lot of girls who couldn't believe this guy got with her."

"Yeah, I can't believe it either," I say.

"She's a witch," Gina tells Marvel.

Marvel only smiles and remains mum.

When the server comes, Gina talks to him as if he's standing on the other side of the gym.

"I'm getting a gigantic steak. I've been dieting to fit into these pants and they're still not really allowing me to breathe right."

The woman taking our order looks very not impressed. I glance over at Marvel, and she has a permanent amused smile on her face. As long as that smile doesn't leave, I'm good with anything that happens tonight. Anything at all.

"Does Marvel know about your spring-break story?" Devon asks.

We've finished our meals and so far have had a fun time talking about everything from school to Devon's crazy family to pretty much every single thing possible about Gina.

But this is not something I want to talk about.

"No."

I say it in a way that clearly says I don't want Marvel to hear about it.

"What story is this?" Marvel asks.

"It's about his trip to Arizona with Taryn."

I shake my head.

"Really?" Gina bursts out. "Let's hear it."

"Let's don't," I say.

"Oh, this sounds interesting," Marvel says. "Yes, definitely, let's hear it."

She still looks completely amused. I look at Devon.

Don't go there.

But I'm outnumbered by two girls. Plus Devon's probably trying to get back at me for getting him into this whole night—or at least for encouraging Gina to get him into it.

"It was last spring break. Brandon drove Taryn to Arizona."

"You *drove* to Arizona? Where in Arizona?"

"Tucson," I tell Marvel. "We took Taryn's car. It was a long drive. The longest drive of my life."

Devon laughs. "He came back looking like he'd been to a funeral."

"I had," I say. "It was a long spring break. Because it was one long week of breaking up."

"Why'd you drive so far?" Marvel asks.

"I wanted to just get out of here," I say.

I don't mention the fact that a few weeks earlier my father had roughed me up really nice. I wanted to get away from home. I also thought maybe the trip would somehow bring me closer to Taryn. Instead it only made me really and truly dislike her.

Or despise her.

"We alternated driving, and it was just—we argued the whole time," I say. "We were staying with her uncle and aunt and they're crazy. I mean—seriously crazy."

"How?" Gina asks.

"They were control freaks. They made us go to bed early, and then the next day they just disappeared. They had these little dogs—ugh, it's painful to think about. We spent more time walking dogs than ever. It was no vacation—walking little poodles and arguing and getting yelled at by this couple who had never had kids and whose skin was orange. Seriously—their skin was orange."

Marvel is laughing. "That sounds like a great time."

"And on the way home, when we'd already broken up and we were both so sick of each other, the car broke down and we had to spend an extra day together. And it wasn't like— oh, we sorta hate each other but we're here and let's make the best of it. Or it wasn't even like people annoyed with each other but finally getting together. We were sick of each other. Period. End of the story."

Gina calls Taryn a rather unfortunate name.

"I have an aunt and uncle who live in Alaska," Marvel jokes.

"I'll gas up the Honda Pilot tonight," I say.

"You were a mess when you came back," Devon says. "For a while even mentioning Taryn's name made him hostile."

"Okay," I say. "Let's talk about Devon."

I don't feel that bad that the story came up, because even Devon doesn't know the half of it. Taryn's just not a good person, inside or out, and I truly realized it on that ill-fated trip.

"Tell me a funny story about Devon," Gina says.

"Okay. Just remember to tell your children this when you're older."

Now Devon is the one shaking his head at my comment.

I don't necessarily have any crazy wild stories about Devon. I just have lots of Devon-being-Devon stories that are funny when you know him and his family.

"Well, one thing about Devon," I say, remembering a good story, "is that he believes in ghosts. Right?"

"I know what you're going to tell."

"He used to believe that the cemetery just up from Sykes Quarry was haunted by some old woman who could be seen roaming around it searching for her lost son."

"I still believe it's haunted," Devon says.

"So one Halloween a few years ago Barton got his cousin to dress up like an old lady and pretend to be a ghost. We went there late at night after trick-or-treating and we spotted this ghost and Devon freaked out."

"I didn't freak out."

"Oh, you freaked out. Completely. He was hysterical."

"He's making this up," Devon tells the girls.

"No way. He totally believed it was the ghost, and he flipped. He ran off and we found him hiding. It took us a while to convince him that it wasn't a ghost he saw."

"I still think that cemetery is haunted," Devon says.

"See?" I laugh.

Gina smiles and reaches over to grab Devon's hand. "Don't worry. I'll protect you from the ghosts out there."

Devon couldn't look more uncomfortable. He looks as if he would rather be in the cemetery this very moment. I love it.

31

"I want you to do me a favor."

The pounding bass of the silly pop song has already made me want to bolt from the gym, but I'm not going anywhere without the lady in white next to me. I nod at her request. She knows I'll do pretty much anything she says, including going out on the dance floor even though I have the rhythm of a walrus.

"Forget about all of this, okay?" she says in a loud voice.

The gym is full, and I've probably already rolled my eyes several times.

"I'm fine."

"You look like your tonsils are being taken out."

"Really? That bad?"

She nods.

"Any way you can make Greg and his circle of studmuffins disappear?" I say.

I saw them earlier and couldn't help wondering what he thought about the prank we pulled. I gave him a nice smile of greeting but suddenly saw my future and the beating I might be getting from these big bodies just standing there like a meeting of Incredible Hulks.

"Don't worry about them," Marvel says.

Of course, they're not the only ones I'm wishing weren't around. There's also Taryn.

Of course, she's in an outfit that's barely there, giving all the guys an eyeful. Yeah, she's hot, but she loves showing it off. And somehow I feel this is for me. She knows I like her in a skirt. She knows that got my attention the first time.

But the fact that it still gets my attention—I mean, that I noticed her looking my way and I looked back at her, several times in fact—I hate. I hate that I'm so predictable. That a girl I completely dislike can still wear a tiny skirt and manage to suck in my attention. And maybe that's another look of disgust that Marvel can see.

"Are we going to dance, sadface?" she asks.

"I'm sorry."

"Imagine this is the one and only time you ever take me to homecoming."

I think about that for a moment. "Well, we're seniors now."

She takes my hand. "Remember this summer? Remember when you kept trying to get me on the dance floor?"

"The dance floor?" I ask.

"The figurative dance floor. You know—you kept asking me out. And I kept turning you down."

"Yeah, I remember."

"Well, I'm not turning you down anymore. Okay?"

She pulls me out onto the dance floor, where the song is

perfect and the lights are perfect and everything is perfect because of the person I'm dancing with. I'm no longer thinking about football hulks or tiny skirts. And I'm the most imperfect dancer out there but it doesn't matter. Not now. Not at this moment.

Because Marvel is right. It's not about anybody else.

It's about her and me and this night we have.

I've never considered myself a romantic. I've never been lost listening to music late at night dreaming and longing. I've never written poetry and never studied paintings and never felt like I could grasp my heart and set it in a balloon only to watch it sail up into the sky. But something about tonight and about being with Marvel and about the way she's acting makes me reconsider everything. I mean *everything*.

Like there's some kind of new world I've suddenly discovered. A part of myself that I didn't know existed. I don't quite know how to sum it up. Yeah, I can say that I really like this girl, that maybe I'm falling in love with her, but there's more to it. There's something far deeper than just that I think she's pretty and fun and I like her.

I think for the first time since meeting Marvel this past summer, since hearing about her awful story with her father and her murdered family, since getting her to hang out and getting in trouble for taking her to Lollapalooza, since hearing her talking to me while I lay in the hospital after my father's drunken car crash . . . Since all of those things, this is the first time I've seen her totally let go. She's the same but she's also so . . . free. That's the word that comes to mind as I watch her dance. She's a good dancer, of course, but it's also just in the way she looks.

The smile. The way her hair seems to dance alongside her with each movement she makes. The way she'll take my hand and lead me instead of me leading her. The way she zones out the rest of the gym and only focuses on me.

Something has changed in how she's acting toward me. She's not pulling away. No.

She's pulling me toward her.

And it's kinda wonderful and kinda scary.

We keep dancing while the music plays, the good songs and the cheesy ones. There hasn't been a slow song yet, just a lot of loud noise. But as we dance, her words suddenly drift up from some kind of lost island they've been stuck on.

"This place is just a trailer for a film, Brandon. Our lives here. Heaven is like the movie. Except there's only one trailer before the movie. And the movie won't ever end."

But I don't want this to be a trailer. I want this—*this*—to be the epic film.

"I don't think I'll ever be ready. Not for what's to come."

But what's going to come? Not tonight, but tomorrow or the next day? I'm afraid because I don't want to leave this moment. This dance floor. This freedom and this free-feeling girl.

"I keep praying for a miracle. That's all. I ask God for one, but it never comes."

But how do I tell Marvel that my miracle has already come? How can I explain to her that I didn't even have to pray for it? It just showed up, walking through the door of a record store.

I'm here and laying all my cards on the table and she knows and she can have every single one.

"I'm going to be there for you. And I hope and I pray that one day you'll find your way out of the cave. I pray that you'll finally see God's light waiting for you."

Why am I remembering all these things now, at this particular moment?

"I heard God talk to me. The same way God talked to Moses through the burning bush. Except in this case, the bush was my house. In this case, it was my life."

I don't want to remember anymore. I just want to take her hands and dance. Forget all the darkness and forget all the God talk and the end-of-the-world stuff. Every little bit of it.

"He said I would be his instrument. He said I shouldn't be afraid, but that I would be used in an incredible way. He said I'd save others from something."

No, I want to stop here. End the song and click to a new track. Please. No more. No, because I know what she's going to say next.

"Then he said I would die being used in this way."

I can't. I won't. No.

Stop it stop this stop it now.

I can't think of this girl not being here anymore. From the beginning she was hinting at it, and finally she just came out and said everything. I would love to forget about this, yet her words continue to haunt me.

I'm going to save you.

That smile, that sweetness, that part of the world that makes it so much better and brighter.

I'll die for you, little girl.

I feel goose bumps because I know it's true. I know I would die for her.

32

It's a nice enough night to be able to use the sunroof on my Honda Pilot. I've driven as far away from Appleton and the school and our homes as possible without Marvel wondering if I'm going to kidnap her. We stop at a golf course about fifteen minutes west of town.

"It's nice to be able to see the stars," Marvel says, leaning up against me while we look up at the sky.

"Yeah."

"Is this where you take all your dates?"

"Yep. You caught me. This is my make-out spot."

"Oh, really?" she says. "I'm sorry—I must have confused this with your stargazing spot."

"They're one and the same."

"Really?" she says. "We'll see about that."

I'm content just to be here with an arm around her.

"Isn't it amazing to think that God created all of this out of nothing?" Marvel says. "That it was just black emptiness before he called it to life? He spoke and this happened."

"It does seem incredible."

"What's incredible is that he made us and allowed us to do our own thing. To make our own decisions."

"Big mistake," I say, half joking.

"No. Big blessing. But of course, we're flawed and sinful. We do things on our own and get in trouble."

"Yeah."

She snuggles against my chest. If she falls asleep I'll let her sleep beside me all night.

"Brandon?"

"That's me."

"I want to tell you something. I've been waiting for the right moment."

"Uh-oh."

"What?"

"Maybe you shouldn't. Maybe not now."

"No, I want to. I need to."

I can't see her face, since her head is on my chest. I can feel her when she's talking and it's a good sensation.

"Remember I texted you that I had something to tell you?"

I'm afraid for the worst. Who knows what she's going to say.

"Everything I've told you—it's still all true. I mean—I still believe in everything. I still believe that . . . that something will happen."

"Maybe and maybe not," I tell her.

'Cause I still believe that maybe I can do something about it.

"But that doesn't mean . . . well, I know what I feel God has—I just—I don't know if I'd call it disobeying or what, but I—I mean I'm not sure . . ."

I move because I want to see her face now. I want to see why she's struggling with telling me this.

"What's wrong?" I ask her, face-to-face now.

Those stars still shine above us like some kind of glorious halo.

"I believe," Marvel says, her bright dark eyes suddenly tearing up. "And I'm okay with it. I'm ready. But I just— I don't think it's too much to ask for a little love. To ask for a little joy. And that's what I choose."

I wipe her tears away with gentle fingers. "Okay."

I'm not totally following her.

"No, Brandon—I'm choosing love. I'm choosing joy." She leans over and kisses me on the lips for a brief moment, then leans back and looks at me. "I choose you."

I want to say something, but my words haven't caught up with my heart. "I'm not sure—"

"I'm not sure, either," Marvel interrupts. "But I know— I love you. I love who you are and I love being around you. And kind of love a little bit of everything about you. Even you on the dance floor. And I don't want to wait because I don't have time to wait. And maybe I shouldn't. Maybe God's told me it's a bad idea but I can't imagine why. Because I know it's good and right. I'll accept whatever God has in store for me. But I just want this—I want—I want you, Brandon."

Then she kisses me. For the first time, she kisses me, like *really* kisses me.

The CD that is playing in the background, the one that Harry gave me, seems to suddenly grow faint, and the star-filled sky above us fades away. I'm lost and locked with

Marvel. I'm kissing her and I'm sinking further and further and have no desire to come up for air.

Of course, I still have to breathe, and of course Marvel isn't going to let her desire rule this moment. Our kiss does finally end, and we're left watching the skies for a little while longer. It's the perfect way to end the night, knowing she's there by my side. Silent, glowing, watchful, just like the stars above.

33

The next morning, I wake up different. I'm not sure how, but I am.

The guy in the mirror still looks the same. Not ugly, not extremely handsome, but suddenly he's got a look and a vibe about him. He resembles a better sort of me.

The morning sunrise and the blue sky feel different. My brothers are less annoying and my father is less threatening and I'm full. I'm bursting. It's kind of crazy and I'd never admit it to anyone other than Marvel. I might even not necessarily tell her all of these feelings because they're a bit overwhelming.

I'm glad to go to church with her. Just Marvel by herself. To sit with her and listen to more of her world. I guess some of it makes sense. I'm learning a little about it and trying not to resist. I don't want to resist the world the way I have for about, oh, seventeen years. I don't want to put up my hands anymore. Whether I'm shielding myself from the blows or deflecting the pain I hold or simply trying not to see.

I want to see clearly, because I like what I see.

Knowing someone loves you is a glorious sort of thing.

"Wish I could spend the whole day with you."

I'm parked in front of her apartment building, waiting to drop her off. It seems like a long time ago when I pulled up yesterday afternoon and saw this vision in white standing there.

"I wish I could invite you in."

I nod. "I wish either of us had a home we could bring each other to."

"You know why I can't."

"Your uncle."

Marvel nods.

"Well, you know why I don't."

"Your father," she says.

"You know, maybe the two of them should get together."

Beat each other up.

"Send them on a trip far, far away."

"Over a cliff," I say, joking but not joking.

"So I'll see you tomorrow then."

"Yeah."

"Maybe I'll hear from you later today."

"Or maybe all day long."

She leans over and gives me a kiss on the cheek. I want more but it's okay.

"Keep in touch," I tell her.

"I will."

I watch her head into the apartment building. I wonder what awaits her. I hope nothing bad.

I'm home barely ten minutes before I'm longing to get back out of the house. Carter is at a friend's, and Alex is upstairs playing video games. Mom is doing laundry and other stuff, so she's upstairs and downstairs and in the basement. Actually, I think she's hiding down there, because Dad is in the family room watching the Bears lose. And we all know that things don't go well if the Bears are losing, whether Dad is "sober" or not.

I've fixed myself a really sad-looking sandwich when I hear a crash from the family room. It sounded like someone ran through a wall. Mom comes into the kitchen, carrying some towels.

"What was that noise?" I ask.

"The Bears are losing."

She doesn't need to say anything more.

If the Bears won and went to the Super Bowl and had Peyton Manning for a quarterback, well, maybe my life would be different. But the Bears are stuck losing and I'm stuck in misery.

I hear some shouted curses.

"Who are they playing?" I ask her.

"Green Bay."

"Say no more."

I seriously need to get out of this house. Fast.

I check the score. Green Bay 42, Bears 10. It's not even the fourth quarter.

"Mom, I have to go out for a while," I call out, but I leave before I know she's heard me.

Devon is glad to see me, but the first thing he asks is how the night ended and if anything happened with Marvel.

"That's none of your business."

"Come on," Devon says. "You forced me to go on that awful date."

"So how's Gina? Have you spoken with her today?"

"Um, no."

"She's nice."

"She never shuts up."

I laugh. "Then you two make the perfect couple."

"You guys left before the night was over."

"It was a lot of fun," I say.

"She sure seems to like you."

"Yeah. It's cool. I think you should ask Gina out again," I say.

"No thanks."

That'll shut him up about girls.

As usual, we play a video game. This is a zombie one that's particularly fun because the zombies are so nasty. They'll be eating livers and brains when you come up on them. Plus their heads explode like juicy watermelons when you shoot them.

"Hey, I meant to tell you . . . remember the warehouse we went to that night? The one with the chimney I had seen piping out smoke?"

"I'm trying to forget about that," I say.

"They still use it. Every Tuesday night."

"And you know this how?" I pause the zombie game for a moment. "Are you still going by there?"

"Yeah. And it's creepy. I still think something's not right about it."

"Dead body in the river creepy? Or glowing ghosts on the back patio creepy?"

"Both." He pauses, then adds, "And don't think I don't hear your sarcasm."

"Good," I say, resuming the game. "I'm telling you, don't mess around with things you don't know about."

"I'm just curious."

"So ask around. Don't go spying at night."

"Want to come?"

"No," I say. "Absolutely not."

"Why not?"

"So we can end up going home and asking a bunch more questions? What do you think you're going to find?"

"That's what I want to know," he says.

"So someone's using a warehouse. So what? It could be a hundred different reasons. *Boring* reasons."

"Involving Otis Sykes?"

"Look—just because this old guy who lives in the woods and owns a quarry happens to be doing weird things—it doesn't mean you should keep spying on him."

"Maybe he's worth spying on," Devon says.

Otis Sykes, the guy the quarry is named after, has for some reason captured my friend's attention ever since Artie Duncan showed up dead in the river.

"Someone told me that building is being used for office space or something," I say.

"It's not true. Nobody is in there," Devon says.

"Ooh. Freaky."

This whole spying-on-people-for-who-knows-what-reason is getting boring.

"Besides looking weird and living by himself in the woods, what else has this Sykes guy done?"

"Don't you think the connection between Artie and Sykes is something?"

I don't say anything, which is saying enough. At least for Devon.

"Yeah, you know what I'm talking about."

"No I don't," I say. "I just keep saying, be careful."

"I am. I will be. Heck—you're in more danger at your house than I am snooping on strangers."

Devon doesn't mean this as some kind of dig. He's just being himself and talking off the top of his head. Besides, he's right. The only reason I'm here is because the Bears are losing and Dad is furious and I know what he can do with that fury. I'm sure he's telling Mom he's not drinking, but I'm just as sure he is. And even if he's not, he can still bite like some wounded wild dog.

Yeah, Devon's right.

"There's one other thing," he says.

"I don't want to hear it."

"I've seen a guy hanging around with Otis."

"Who?"

Devon pauses, so I stop playing again and look at him and see his grim face.

"Carlos. Marvel's uncle."

34

I drive past the actual turnoff twice. It's barely more than a dirt road heading into the woods. But my GPS is leading me this way, so I turn in and keep driving.

I'm about two hundred yards away when I see a large rectangular barn lit up in the dark of night. Suddenly I imagine a keg and a bunch of guys sitting around drinking beer. I've been to parties like that before. The only difference is I usually knew the guys. The only person I'm expecting to know here is Seth, and I don't know him very well.

The October night is cool, and my denim jacket seems extra thin. I'm trying not to think about what a bad idea this could be. What do I know about this except that an odd kid from my school invited me?

And I'm trying to be a friend to him.

Several vehicles are parked outside the barn, mostly trucks. Blue-collar-worker sort of trucks. Maybe this is some kind of union meeting. Who knows.

I stay in my car for a moment, wondering whether I should really go inside. At least there's light behind the doors. If it was completely dark, I'd get out of here. Before I saw fairy lights or a herd of cats.

Come on, Brandon.

I picture Marvel in my head and know that in some way I'm doing this for her. On the off chance that maybe, somehow, this has to do with her voice and her premonition and her whatever from God.

Maybe God will show up at this party one way or another.

I get out of the Honda and look up to the sky, wishing I could be watching the stars again with Marvel.

The first thing I notice about the guy who greets me at the door is his neck. It looks extra long, like someone tried to grab his head and couldn't quite pull it off. There are several veins that look like underground cables or power cords. And on one side, right above his camouflage T-shirt, is some kind of tattoo. Not a subtle one, either, but a big one, something that looks like a dagger or a cross.

Oh, and another thing. He's got a really great mustache, the kind they wore in the seventies.

He's styling like Marvel with his seventies vibe.

"Who are you?"

The only vibe this guy gives off is danger.

"I'm, uh, Brandon Jeffrey. Seth Belcher told me about the—about coming out here."

I'm not sure if I should say *party*, because so far, standing at the half-closed door, all I can see is this mass of muscles and veins. He gives me a really awful sort of look, the kind someone might give to a set of clothes hanging on a mannequin. The kind that makes it look like you're deciding what to do with the thing you're looking at.

"Jeremy—I invited him."

The door opens fully and I see Seth. He's wearing his kamikaze bandana along with some kind of ninja outfit. I'd laugh, but Jeremy doesn't seem to be the joking type. He moves over to let me in, then looks out to the darkness beyond.

"Anybody with you?" he asks.

He's got a weird sort of accent. Southern with a bit of Chicago.

"No."

"He's cool," Seth says. "He's the one I told you about."

The guy shuts the door and locks it. The barn is wide with nothing in it except for what appear to be stalls toward the back. I see six or seven guys standing around, holding beer, smoking, and talking.

This isn't a high school party.

The guys—and they're all men—look like bikers or truckers. Maybe that's a generalization, since I don't encounter many bikers or truckers, but the leather vests and leather Harley coat jump out at me. Another guy is wearing a cap with profanity front and center on it. And a big, big guy who looks like Jabba the Hut in a denim jacket is definitely smoking something other than a cigarette.

This is totally shady.

"So what's your story?" Jeremy asks me.

He's got the most distant look I've ever seen. It sorta goes right through you, like he's there but not there. Or like you're not really there.

"I go to Appleton High with Seth."

Jeremy nods, looks around the room, then looks at Seth.

"The soccer player?" he asks.

"Yeah," Seth says.

"Okay."

Jeremy walks away in some kind of slow, zombie-like walk. If someone was walking like that in a Walmart I'd think something was seriously wrong with him. Seth nods to me and actually looks halfway charming compared to the grim guy there.

"You find it okay?"

"Yeah," I say. "I guess I forgot to dress up."

"I bring this out every now and then. They think I'm crazy, but that's okay."

"Seth—who are these people?" I ask him in a whisper. "Like how do you know them?"

"From Jeremy. You want a beer?"

I don't, but I nod simply because I don't want to be rude or considered a prude. He leads me over to a wooden barrel full of ice and pulls out a couple cans of beer.

"Listen—you might see some weird things tonight."

I think of the dark house and the creepy vibes Devon got from being there. I'd really prefer not to see any weird things tonight. Or ever.

"Like what?"

Seth takes a sip from his beer. "Just—stuff. These guys can get a bit rowdy."

They're just talking, scanning the room, chilling out. Seems pretty tame to me.

"What are they going to do? Dance?"

Seth shakes his head. "No. Fight."

I wait for a laugh or a punch line, but nothing comes. Seth is serious. I open my beer but have no desire to drink it.

I really just want to go back home. I don't need to be hanging around here.

I so want to ask him if Artie Duncan ever hung around with these guys.

I could imagine any of the men in this room killing Artie. And I'm at a party with all of them. Awesome.

35

"Five knuckles. That's all you can use."

The odd party I'm attending has become a circle of about ten guys. Nobody has talked to Seth or me for the last hour. Seth drinks beer and occasionally disappears into one of the stalls in the back. Maybe to smoke a joint or something, I don't know. He seems like his typical odd self, barely answering my questions, standing there for minutes without saying a word.

But in the last few minutes something's changed. It's like a light switch went on, and all the disinterested guys suddenly took notice. A guy smaller than me, who looks ordinary in every way, gets everybody's attention and is talking to the group at the center of the circle. Jeremy is standing next to him and so is the big guy in a leather vest.

I'm still trying to comprehend his whole "five knuckles" comment.

Jeremy stares at the bigger guy, who starts to jog up and down and move around like a boxer at a fight.

I've seen the movie *Fight Club* and even heard of one that existed in Russia. But here in Appleton, Illinois?

And is Seth a part of this? Is he fighting these older guys?

"The rules are simple. First person who goes to the ground and stays on the ground loses."

Another horrible thought comes to me: what if they're expecting me to fight?

I feel nauseous from all the questions going off inside my head.

"Jeremy, Bernard. You guys ready?"

Both men nod. Jeremy puts his left hand behind his back. His arms are all solid muscle, but the other guy—Bernard—has to weigh twice as much as he does.

I've seen fights online and see some stupid wannabe fights, but I've never seen something up close. It's kind of thrilling, but at the same time I'm freaked out.

The ordinary guy—dressed plainly in jeans and button-down shirt—walks away from the middle of the circle. There are some howls and cheers now. The guys are into this.

Jeremy and his thick mustache size up Bernard. Then he puts his right fist up, as if he's going to hit the guy on his cheek. Bernard defends it by putting his hand up along the side of his face. Then in the fastest move I've ever seen, Jeremy plants his fist straight up on the guy's chin. I hear something crack. Then he begins to punch downward in a flurry of jabs, down down down against Bernard's forehead and nose. The big guy goes down immediately, and I see a triangle of blood gushing from his nose. His legs buckle and he falls on the dirt and stays there.

The reaction is intense. There are groans and ows and laughter and curses. Everybody seems to love what they just saw, but they are also quietly freaked. As if maybe they're thinking, *That could be me.*

Bernard starts to cry. A grown man—a big, big grown man—is crying and holding his busted nose. Jeremy just stands there over him and shakes his head. Soon he's howling in laughter, the sort of *muwahahaha* that I only see someone putting online in a FB or Twitter post.

Seth glances at me and I see something on his face. Something that is scary to look at.

It's a sort of giddy, delightful glee.

"I better go."

It's been about ten minutes since the fight that lasted a whole twenty seconds, if that. The guys are standing around again, talking, drinking beer, and smoking. Seth disappears with Jeremy for a moment and then comes back, his eyes glassy.

"Sorry it wasn't longer," Seth says. "I didn't realize Jeremy was up tonight."

"Is this like some kind of fight club or something?" I ask.

Seth nods, laughing. I can tell he's high. "Yeah, something like that. But Brad Pitt isn't coming out of the stalls anytime soon."

"How often do you guys do this?"

"Often enough."

I want to ask if he fights, but then again I don't want to get invited to join in. Maybe they'd make us fight since we're the same age. I just want to get out of here.

"You interested in smoking a bong?" Seth asks.

I shake my head.

"Thought you liked that stuff."

I shrug and change the subject.

"It's just—I better go. I didn't tell my parents where I'd be."

"Yeah."

He's in another world by now.

I look around and see Bernard sitting on a chair, holding a T-shirt against his busted nose. He's laughing and joking around with the guys like someone who just had a good workout.

"They're a pretty good group," Seth says.

I nod but will have to say I respectfully disagree. The only person I'd want to invite to this strange party is my father. Maybe he could do the five-knuckles-thing with Jeremy.

"I'll see you around, okay?"

"Oh, wait. Jeremy wants to say something."

Long-and-tattooed-neck ends up walking me to the car.

"Not every day you see something like that, huh?" he asks in his southern Chicago slow drunken drawl.

"Not exactly."

He laughs and curses and claps me on the shoulder. The blow kills.

"Seth likes you. And I like Seth. He's an odd duck. So if he digs you, that's cool. But you listen. Nobody needs to know about this place or this party. You get it?"

"Yeah, sure. Nobody."

"Even your friends. That tall one with the big hair. Keep him away, okay?"

"Yeah."

I start to open my door when he puts a hand on it and keeps it closed.

"And listen, *Brandon*. Nobody likes people looking into other people's business. You got that? 'Cause that makes you want to do the same. To get into *your* business. And nobody needs to get into your business, right? You got enough to handle, right? *Especialmente con tu novia linda.*"

He tilts his head just to make sure I caught that last line.

I gotta know my Spanish better.

"Yeah," I say.

I don't know if he's actually talking about someone named Linda or if that's Spanish for something. But I get it. I know what he's talking about and that's good enough for me.

"Stay cool, my brother," Jeremy says, opening the door and then shutting it after I'm inside.

The drive away from the barn might be the most relieved moment of my life. *Ever.*

36

This is one of those nights when I could see my father waiting
up for me and using five knuckles on my rib cage. The Bears
lost, which is bad. But the way they lost—I hear a sports com-
mentator on the car radio talking about how bad the defense
and the quarterback and the coach and even the fans were,
and I realize that things at home could be ugly.

When I pull into my driveway, it's a little after ten. The
door to the garage is open and the lights are on. Bad signs.

I shut off the car and climb out, wondering if Dad saw
me and if I can make it inside without being stopped. The
detached garage has been sort of like an office for my father,
his private work space—especially in the last year and a half
since he lost his job. He doesn't really "work" out there on
anything but a six-pack, as far as I can tell. And it's too messy
to ever actually get a car inside.

I feel a blast of cold and I shiver, keeping one eye out for
any sort of movement within . . .

I blink, then suddenly I see the garage in flames. Yellow

and orange and red intertwined like snakes dancing. Blazing, furious flames covering the garage.

I cower, bending over and covering my face in shock and horror. My eyes burn for a moment and then . . .

It's gone.

It's the good ole garage, the one my father hides out in, the one with a hundred tools that are never used.

I look around to see if I'm losing my bearings or my brain or something.

What'd I just see?

It's another of those weird things that have happened ever since I met Marvel. Most have happened when I've been with her, or after seeing her. The weird dream-slash-nightmares and dream-slash-visions that look and feel so real. I've never had much of an imagination, so I have no idea where these are coming from.

They came right after Artie died too.

I met Marvel the same day that Artie's body was found. I wonder if it's a coincidence. I wonder if this vision of a blazing fire is just some random thing.

I felt the fire and my eyes burned 'cause it was real.

I breathe in and then slowly let it out. I don't want to go in there, but something inside tells me I need to. That I have to.

I close my eyes again, this time for longer. I wonder what Marvel would do.

She'd go in. But she'd be praying as she went.

"God help me," I say.

I don't know if it's a real prayer or just a sort of desperate heaven-help-us sort of thing. But I walk into the garage.

I find my father crumpled on the floor by a table that holds junk and tools and a little television that is playing. A stool is overturned and Dad is sideways on the floor as if someone knocked him out.

It takes me about thirty seconds to spot the vodka bottle, barely hidden behind a can of gasoline on the floor underneath the table.

I gotta get out of here—it's stifling hot and I'm sweating already.

I'm ready to head into the house when a steady buzzing sound penetrates my consciousness. Fear can silence everything—the sound of a hurricane maybe or a semi driving toward you or maybe even the voice of God. Fear can make every single thing in your life pause and go silent. That's what happened when I saw Dad on the ground.

I'm not afraid of his being dead. I'm afraid of him waking up and catching me here spying on him, seeing him sprawled out like that. I'm afraid he'll beat me in the face because he's embarrassed.

But that noise . . .

I turn toward it and see the orange grills of an old space heater under the wooden worktable.

Inches away from a paint can full of old rags. Inches away from the bottle of vodka. Oh, and just a few feet away from the gasoline can.

And from my father. My drunk, passed-out failure of a father who's just a few feet away from obvious death.

You could walk out of the garage right now, Brandon. Walk out and do nothing.

I think of the time Dad struck me in face with the bottle of booze. The hundreds of things he's said to me. I think of—

Act, you idiot.

And I do. I grab the gas and the paint cans and set them outside. Then I unplug the heater and move it out from underneath the table. I throw the vodka bottle into a recycling can.

Then I try to wake Dad and get him back into the house. I help him to his feet, even though they're wobbly and bent at the knee, and half carry him inside. He mumbles, but in this condition he's harmless.

I slide him across the kitchen floor, trying not to make any noise. We get to the family room, where Alex and Carter are watching television.

"A little help here," I say.

They look up and don't have to ask what's wrong. They help me get him on the long couch.

"You guys should check on him more often."

"We didn't know where he was," Alex says.

"I thought he was upstairs," Carter says.

They don't realize that I might have just saved Dad's life.

The funny thing—well, not funny but sad—is that Dad is going to wake up tomorrow and not have any idea either.

It's not sad, it's tragic.

But then I realize that's not right. Dad dying in the garage would have been tragic.

I think of those three words I said, the ones asking God for some help. As I head back outside to turn off the lights of the garage and clean up a little more, I say three more.

"Thank you, God."

37

I text Marvel around eleven but don't get a response. I wish I could hear just a word from her. Some little piece of joy I could have before going to bed. Before shutting my eyes and seeing who knows what.

Something makes me think of Marvel's blog, so I go check it and see a new post from today. It's got a picture of a young girl twirling in a field of flowers.

FOREVER

Tonight I dance again like a little girl
The clouds swirl silently in the sky
The full moon standing and smiling like a proud parent
I lift up my hands and thank you, God
I praise you for the gifts so abundant and so rich
So wonderful
The melodies and the words remind me
Not so long ago when life was good
When life was still so bright

When I trusted you and when you didn't let go
I dance knowing you still hold my hand
You still spin me around
You still grip me in your arms
You still hold me high
I will be forever a little girl
Standing before her heavenly Father
With fear and wonder
And with a never-ending sense of joy

I read the blog several times. It's a crazy awesome thing to know that she's writing this because of me, because of something I did. Because of me being me. It's an amazing thing to know that I'm bringing someone out there—someone like Marvel—such joy. Never knew that was actually possible.

It's a weird thing, too, seeing her writing about stuff like this—stuff of joy—especially since she's talking about God the *Father*. I don't get it. I want to ask her how in the world she can believe like that. I would love to have that kind of faith. I have no doubt it's real. Doesn't mean I believe God is up there or that he's in any way like a father. But her faith and belief—those things are real.

I think of my father passed out on the couch. Then I think of Marvel's father who torched all of them.

Yet she survived.

She survived for what reason? So she could do what?

I don't want to think about that now. I just want to remember the joy she's writing about.

I want to remember dancing with her and looking up at the stars and knowing someone's by my side.

38

It's weird the way love can make you forget about pretty much everything else. It's a cold and rainy second week of October outside, yet things have never felt so warm and bright in my life. It's all Marvel's doing, of course. It's a wonderful thing waking up knowing there's someone out there who's thinking about you, probably wondering how you are, caring deeply about you for no other reason than that she can.

It's enough to make me forget about things like Artie Duncan and the other dead girl from the summer. The football players and Seth Belcher. My father and everything about him. Taryn and her snotty self. Devon and his crazy fantasies. Even weird visions.

There's a nice routine to my life, and it pretty much revolves around Marvel.

The first part begins when I pick her up. The day officially starts when I see her standing there, smiling when I drive up, usually wearing something smart and brilliant. She greets me in different ways. One morning with a kiss. Another with an egg sandwich. Another with a page of writing she wants to read to me for her English class.

I used to be concerned that I'd be "that guy" following Taryn around like a puppy dog, but when it comes to Marvel I don't care. I am that guy and I do follow her around.

So far she hasn't made any close girlfriends, though it's obvious a lot of girls like her. Not Taryn, of course, who seems to be hating her more with each week. But Marvel ignores that. She hangs with me and the guys at lunch, and then after school I'll take her home or to the record store where I'll stick around if I don't have soccer practice or a game.

There are no more words spoken about coming apocalypses. No premonitions or omens. And I've even stopped having those weird dreams.

This is what it feels like to be a senior who is "smitten" and has no serious issues to worry about.

For now.

That voice lingers and reminds me every now and then, but I ignore it. And I'll keep doing that. For now.

"Hey, Brandon, I gotta show you something."

Devon is holding his phone and looking strange. Looking sort of angry, actually, which is unusual for him.

"What is it?"

"It's your ex." And he calls Taryn a bad name. Like the worst thing you can ever call a girl. Again, something new for Devon, especially on a Tuesday morning.

"Okay, so what'd Taryn do now?" I can't help but smile,

because it's probably something totally random that's got Devon worked up.

He gives me the phone. "Check that out. Taryn's Facebook page."

I touch the screen and see Taryn's glowing, wonderful fake smile as she poses in her bikini top in the little picture in the corner. But I don't think that's what Devon wants me to see.

Her status, dated last night, reads:

This is messed up. Wonder if she brought all the bad stuff that's been happening to Appleton with her.

I have a sinking feeling inside when I see a link to a newspaper article.

> CHICAGO—A 38-year-old man burned down his home in Humboldt Park Tuesday night. He was armed with an AK-47 rifle, apparently upset about family issues.

I want to throw up. Like seriously spew all over the hallway floor.

I can see my hand shaking.

> Miraculously, the older daughter managed to escape . . .

I look up at Devon. Now I understand his anger. I nod as he curses at Taryn again.

> Alonso Garcia had a history of domestic abuse . . .

I look around, scared that Marvel is going to suddenly stumble upon us looking at this.

The surviving daughter is now in the custody of her
aunt and uncle.

"Unbelievable," I say.

"Read the comments," Devon says.

There are twenty-nine of them already. It's a lot of Taryn's
friends agreeing with her and saying things like "Messed up"
and "Crazy." But then Taryn gets back on.

**Who does Marvel think she is anyway with all those weird
outfits? Jennifer Lopez or something?**

Just in case nobody knew who the article was talking
about, *now* they do.

I instantly start heading down the hallway to find Taryn.

"Hey, Brandon," Devon shouts out.

"What?"

"My phone."

"Oh, yeah."

I give it back before resuming my hunt for the witch who
decided to do a little cyber-bullying last night.

I catch up with her right before she can go into her class.

"Stay out here," I tell Taryn, standing in front of her and
blocking her way.

"Brandon, I'm late."

I tell her exactly what I think about her.

"How could you say that stuff about Marvel on Facebook?
Or ever?"

"You're kinda hot when you get angry and start with lan-
guage like that."

She rolls her eyes and tries to move around me, but I block
her way again. I've never wanted to hit a girl before, though

there were times when we were dating that I really *should* have hit Taryn. An image of my father pops into my mind, and I know I've got a little bit of him in me. I'd never actually hit her. But I can't help feeling like I want to slap the fire out of her face.

"Do you know how messed up that is?" I ask her.

"Then unfriend me."

"Someone else showed it to me."

"So? What's the big deal? It was a news article."

"And you're suggesting that her *losing* her whole family—her father killing them all—and then her moving to Appleton has *anything* to do with the stuff that's happened around here?"

I curse again and wonder if any teachers are going to come out of their rooms to see what's happening.

"The prince to the princess's rescue," Taryn says.

"Take this down now. I mean now."

Her eyes roll again, and I want to permanently make them roll way back in her skull. I can't believe the evil inside this girl's heart.

"What is wrong with you? Are you really that awful a person?"

"You wouldn't know, would you?" she says.

I'd like to take those blonde locks she's brushing back and shave them all off and give them to a girl who doesn't have hair. Then I'd like to go back in time and punch myself and make sure I don't ever go out with her. Ever.

"You take it down now or I'm going to tell someone."

"Ooh, I'm so scared."

"You're getting worse," I tell her. "You've never been like this."

"I'm growing up," Taryn says. "You should try it. It's a tough world out there."

"Then don't take something beautiful and try to break it."

The witch only laughs. "She's already broken. You just can't see it. You're too stupid."

With this Taryn walks away.

A feeling of pure rage burns in me. I shiver because it's scary, this feeling I have. Like a protective mother animal. I clench my fists and my jaw and anything else I can clench as I go to my next class.

I only hope Marvel hasn't seen the post yet.

39

"You need some more music to listen to," Marvel tells me later that afternoon on the way home.

It's after soccer practice but she stayed behind to wait for me. So far she's not mentioned anything about Taryn's Facebook post; I'm pretty positive she didn't see it. She hasn't acted like anything other than her upbeat self.

"It's not like you live an hour away from school."

"Still. For someone who works at a record store—"

"Yeah, yeah. I know. Are you telling me you don't like talking to me?"

"We can do both," she says. "And the radio just doesn't work for me."

"Bring whatever music you want."

"You find something."

"Oh, come on. We already have a nice selection of songs on a CD."

"Someone else made that. I want you to make me a playlist."

I sigh. "Talk about pressure."

"No pressure. Just find songs that remind you of me."

"I have a lot of homework, you know."

"Well, I did mine this afternoon. Waiting on you."

She laughs and then places her hand in mine. I can steer with my left hand.

The drizzle outside is enough to be annoying and cause me to use the windshield wipers periodically. The cold is enough to make me wish I'd worn a coat. The weather is enough to have made soccer practice extra exciting.

When we get to the stop sign just before her apartment parking lot, I hear a sigh.

"That sounds like you're excited to go home."

"Is there a place we can just . . . live?"

"I can look into some cheap places. But you know— on my salary . . ."

"I don't like being with those two."

I turn into the lot but stop before getting to the place where I usually let her out.

"Everything okay? With your aunt and uncle?"

She sighs and puts her hands in between her legs, then stretches. "No. But it never has been since I first got here."

"But why?"

The only thing I've ever really understood from Marvel is that her aunt doesn't really like her and her uncle maybe likes her *too* much. In a not-so-likable way.

"I just always—I don't know—I'm always sort of waiting and wondering when something awful is going to happen. When I'm going to open the door and find my aunt in there with a loaded gun. Or my uncle hovering over my bed."

If I'd had a conversation with a girl in my class a year ago and she'd said something like this, I would have simply said, *Nice knowing you, nutcase, but see ya!* But of course, I understand what Marvel's talking about. I understand her past and her present. I understand the reality of what she's talking about. Doesn't make it any better, however.

"Do you ever think—the reason why you're here—that it has something to do with them?"

Marvel looks out the window toward the building. It's nearly dark outside, so I can mainly see the outline of her face in the shadows of the car.

"Sometimes," she says. "But I don't know. I've stopped trying to figure it out. I've asked God to show me his will when the time is right."

I take her hand and get her to look back at me. "You think it's God's will for us to be together?"

"No."

"That's not good then, is it?"

She shrugs. "It feels good when I'm with you."

"Maybe it is and you just don't realize it," I say, moving over to kiss her.

For a few moments we enjoy this sanctuary. I lose a little bit of reality touching her lips. I could keep kissing her all night.

"I should go," she says.

Every part of my body doesn't want to stop.

"I know," I tell her.

"You know that—even though this whole thing—the you and me—there can't be any—any of *that*."

I touch the side of her face. I love doing this, just to feel how soft it is, just to make sure she's real.

"I know."

"I mean it, Brandon."

"I know."

She looks at me and thinks about what she's going to say. "I can have the best intentions, and I can want to do good, but I have to be careful. I have to be in constant prayer and always remind myself how easy it might be."

"I'm not asking for anything here," I tell her.

"I know you aren't. It's only natural, especially when everybody you know seems to be having sex without much of a care in the world. But I care. I don't want to because I know it's wrong."

This makes me a bit sad, not because of what she's saying but because of Taryn. Because I lost my virginity to this girl that I can't even stand to be in the same school building with. I can't take that back, either. That stamp was punched in the passport of my life and will always be there, no matter where I go and what I do.

"You're not upset, are you?" she asks about my silence.

"No. No, not at all. It's hard not to continually be in awe of how you are . . . you."

"Don't. It's not me. It's not. And besides. I might say things—I told you all summer long we couldn't be together, and look at me now."

"I know." I smile.

"Don't give me that."

"What?"

"That look."

"Why?"

"Just because," Marvel says.

"Because why?"

"Because—it's—it's dangerous."

"Oh, please."

She leans over and gives me a good-bye peck on the lips.

"Stop messing with my mind like that," I tell her.

"I like that you don't realize certain things about yourself."

"Like what?"

Marvel only shakes her head and then tells me she's got to go. She leaves me still wondering what she's talking about. Still curious if I really do have that effect on her.

Still buzzing with the thought that one day, we could make a big awful glorious mistake with each other.

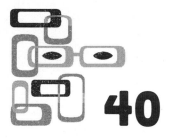

40

Hey Brandon.

At first I think the late-night text is from Marvel, but it's Devon.

Yeah.

You free Friday?

So far I don't have any plans, but I have an idea what Devon wants to do.

No, I write.

There's somewhere we gotta go.

No, not we. Just you.

He doesn't reply for a while, so I add, **You should let it go.**

Why?

It's an obsession, I text.

So is Marvel.

I guess he has a point, even though they're different. Marvel is real and something I can physically touch. Someone I want to keep touching. This thing Devon is chasing is some kind of faint idea. The idea of strange things happening, things that somehow have to do with Artie.

It's two different things, I text.

Maybe to you.

Why are you so consumed with this? I ask him.

Can you go or not?

No.

OK.

I've seen Seth a few times this week but haven't actually talked to him. Today I see him eating by himself at a table on the edge of the cafeteria. I head over to say hi.

"You remember my name," he says with a bit of an edge in his voice.

I laugh. "Hey—I said hi the other day and you didn't say anything."

He's got little containers for all his food. I see some lasagna, some carrots and dip, chips. He's got a whole meal going on here.

"I figured you probably got all freaked out going to the barn the other night," he says between chewing his food.

"Come on. You gotta admit—that was a bit out there, you know?"

Cold eyes look at me with no reaction. "No, I don't know."

"I'm not judging or anything. But those guys—they're like thirty-year-old biker dudes."

"They're good guys. Not like the jerks around here."

"Don't put me in that category," I say.

"You're not."

I look over and see Devon and Frankie waiting on me.

"You can go," Seth says. "Your charity work is done for the day."

"Look—you can sit with us anytime."

"Yeah, right. I'm fine by myself. I enjoy it."

"Having any football troubles?"

Seth glances around while he shakes his head no. "They're laying off."

Maybe Greg is just bored. But ever since painting his car, I've wondered what might happen next.

"Did they ever do anything after the party? The one where you busted what's-his-face's nose?"

"No."

"I'd still watch out if I were you."

"I do. And I got backups now to help."

On the way to class I see Greg and Sergio and some other football players. They're talking and laughing, and Greg watches me with a moronic grin on his face. Like he's got something planned. I don't know what, but he's just got that look.

"I do. And I got backups now to help."

That's a bomb waiting to detonate. I can just see Seth getting beat up and then calling in those psycho dudes to come mess up half the football team.

Yeah, um, sorry, but we're going to have to cancel "Friday Night Lights" because half the team is in the hospital.

A minute later I see Taryn with her friends, and it's like she's Greg's evil twin sister. She's standing there watching me and smiling and whispering.

There's almost two thousand kids that go to this high school, and yet I'm still hounded almost on a daily basis by people like Greg and Taryn. I know they *want* to be seen by everyone. But I'd rather have a week pass where I can simply walk around in peace. Where I can enjoy knowing that the one and only person worth seeing is just a locker away.

"You really need to take the ACT this month."

Mrs. Bauer is maybe the best guidance counselor I could have. There are a few who are total nightmares. Not encouraging, but rather condemning, nagging jerks. Having one of them would be like having my father as a guidance counselor. But Mrs. Bauer is laid-back. She never goes overboard with dates and deadlines and The Future.

"I haven't even started to study for it. Can't I take it in December?"

"Yes, that's an option."

"It's not like I'm going to try to get into Princeton or anything."

"And why not?" she asks, her cheery face breaking into a smile.

"Oh, I don't know. It could be because I'd be a total miserable failure there."

"You're going to do great *wherever* you go."

I tell her that my one and only goal is to get far, far away.

"How are things with your parents?"

Mrs. Bauer knows I can't stand my father and that I've had some issues with my parents, but that's it. I've never shared too much detail, especially about the way my dad has hit me . . . but I think sometimes she can read between the lines.

"No major drama lately."

"Do you talk to either of them about college?"

"Yeah," I say. "My mom is on me. I know I gotta get going. I will."

"Not everybody needs to know exactly what their life's plan and purpose are when they're seventeen."

I laugh. "I know some kids who knew those things freshman year. They were practicing for the ACT even then."

"Everybody's different."

I think of Seth.

Wonder what sort of requirements there are to become a ninja warrior?

Then I think of Marvel and how she never talks about those things. Stuff like college and a career and all that.

"Trust me," Mrs. Bauer says. "You'll blink and it'll be here before you know it."

"College."

"College. A corporate job. Kids. Life doesn't stop."

I nod.

It stops whenever I'm with Marvel.

But how long will I continue to be around her? That's the question I need an answer to.

41

"Okay. So I want to do something I've never done."

Marvel smiles, remembering telling me those same words just a month ago.

"Well, I don't know, Mr. Jeffrey, jet-setter."

"Hardly," I tell her. "Surprise me. You have an hour."

She shakes her head. "Nope."

"What?"

"I had a feeling you might say something like that. So I'm ready. We're going now."

I've been working with Marvel at the record store this Saturday. Or more accurately, she's been working and I'm doing what I spent the summer doing: hanging out and not getting paid. So we had already sort of agreed that we would do something later tonight. But when I tried to pull her surprise-me game on her, Marvel was ready.

She's seemed ready for everything ever since I met her.

She tells me where to drive, and I follow her instructions. It's only a little after seven. Soon I find us in Geneva, and she's telling me to park in the parking garage close to the train station.

"I have a feeling where this is going."

"No you don't," Marvel tells me. "And it's a good thing I'm finally learning my way around."

"You know—I *have* taken the train before."

"We both have," she says. "Transportation doesn't count."

"Okay."

Like I'm going to stop this in any sort of way. If she leads me to a McDonald's in Chicago, I'm going to tell her it's the first time I've entered those golden arches and the very first time I've discovered a delicacy called the Big Mac.

"Do you think there will be trains in heaven?" she asks once we've sat down next to each other on the Metra.

"I've never thought of that."

The reality is that I've never thought of heaven ever. Yet time and time again, Marvel brings it up. Not in a magical fairy tale sort of way but in a "hey, so this thing that's very real, what do you think about it?" sort of way. And that's kind of cool.

"I know there's the whole angels-floating-in-air thought, but that's not what it's going to be about. I read a great book on heaven a few years ago, and it made me think about it in a very real sense. It didn't say things would definitely be like this or that, but it offered ideas that made logical sense."

"Like why animals would be there?" I say, trying to be silly.

"Yeah. That's one thing. And doing the things we love. Like music. I love music. And of course music will be there."

"I guess I'd need to learn hymns."

"You think God would make things like guitars and drums and keyboards to only let us sing hymns for all of eternity?"

Another question I've never thought of and have no answer for.

"I like imagining some of the great songs of all time—the great pop songs—reimagined in heaven. Put into proper perspective."

"I think some songs wouldn't make the cut."

I list off a few suggestive silly songs from the past year.

"But maybe—possibly—they can be tweaked. Because God made music. Music is a good thing."

"You've never heard me sing," I joke.

The rumble of the train is steady and there are few people in our car. It's nice, like we have this train all for ourselves.

"I remember taking the 'L' when we lived downtown. Riding on it with my sister."

"Mirage, right?"

She nods and gives me a sad, reflective smile. "She loved going on the train, even if it was for only a ten-minute ride. I think it represented something amazing for her."

"What do you mean?"

"Freedom," Marvel says. "From our parents. From our lives."

"I'm sorry," I say immediately.

It just slips out; I can't help it.

"You don't have to be."

"I know, I'm sorry—I mean I'm sorry for saying that, it's just—"

"It's okay," she tells me, taking my hand and holding it. "Can I ask you something? A favor?"

"Yeah."

"Don't apologize or become awkward when I talk about my family—my mama, Mirage. You don't have to. I don't want them to *not* be remembered because of what the enemy did to them."

I nod but don't ask her the question in my head.

What the enemy did? Is that her father? Or someone else?

"Tell me about your sister."

For a second Marvel's eyes wander and she is still, as if remembering this really awesome moment that can't help but make you smile.

"Mirage was the little fighter I never was. She called out my parents. My father hated her. He hated her because she was just like he was. She had his DNA. But she also had my mother in her, and that made her wonderful. She wanted to protect me. And if she'd been older—she would've. She *could've*."

I *so* want to say "sorry" again but I don't. I let it go.

"When she was really little I thought that having a younger sister would be annoying, that I'd have to take care of her, but it was the opposite. She was amazing. I loved who she was turning out to be. More athletic than I was. More charming. A little more of everything. I soon let it go, the thought of having to protect her. But of course . . ."

And the tears come. Of course. I can't imagine them not coming.

For a few minutes Marvel leans against me and cries.

I think of her father, and of my father, and the anger builds again. Just like it did when I saw the ridiculously stupid post Taryn put about Marvel on Facebook. I want to stand in the way of all of this. Of those idiots and those evil souls. I want to just stand there and let whatever happens, happen.

Beat me down, I don't care—you're not getting to them.

If only I could have been there for Marvel's sister.

But I'm here for you. I'm here for you and I promise I'll stand in the way of anybody. Anybody.

I don't want to talk about heaven, because we're here. We're here right now riding a train from Geneva to Chicago, not the angelic train to Euphoria Station 101. This is real and she's beside me and I don't want her seeing whatever awaits in heaven.

"I can't imagine heaven feeling better than this," I tell her as I hold her. "This train, being here with you. This is heaven for me."

Her tear-filled eyes look up and she smiles. "Have I ever told you I really like you?"

"No. Tell me again."

"I've got a big-time crush on you, Brandon Jeffrey."

"Well, I think my crush crushes yours, Marvella Garcia."

She smiles, wiping her eyes.

"You know something?"

"What?" I ask.

"I like it when you say my name. My full name."

"Okay, then I'll say it every time I talk to you, Marvella."

"No, I mean it."

"I mean it too, Marvella."

"You're also very funny."

"I try to be, Marvella. Or should I say Berry?"

She laughs. "Yes. Forever Berry."

Then she surprises me with a kiss. Because, of course, every kiss from Marvel is a surprise.

"Thank you, Graham. Thank you for listening and for always figuring out the right words to say."

"Right words? I don't know about that."

"Always," she answers. "I mean that."

Does the city always look this alive? This big? This happy? This wonderful? I don't know, but I know it's all of those things and more. It's like a giant Christmas tree that's been in hiding my whole life and it's suddenly sprung up out of the dark and is doing a mad little dance.

We get off the train and walk out of the building into this fresh breath of air. Cars, adults, lights, busyness, plans, and people all doing their thing. And there in the midst stand Marvel and me.

"It's up to you," I tell her.

But she already knows where we're going.

In some ways, it's like she's known that all along. From the very first time we met.

And the night suddenly twirls around my finger like some endless string changing colors every few circles it makes.

There is a steady breeze going through the buildings, reminding us of the coming cold. Reminding us of the chill outside. So it forces us to walk sideways, leaning on each other.

We get a cab, and Marvel gives the driver an address. I don't know where we're going and she doesn't tell me. But in the backseat we sit close and hold hands and watch the lights all around us blink and spin and turn and glow.

I swear I've never had thoughts like this. Never had cousins of thoughts like this. But they keep showing up like a strange family reunion.

"Trust me," she says.

I swear I'd follow her over the edge of Niagara Falls. I'd be holding her hand for dear life but I'd be okay.

I wonder where we're headed. Navy Pier. The Shedd Aquarium. The beach. Grant Park. Some great pizza place.

Yeah. Chicago.

"Stop trying to guess where we're going. I can see you doing that from here."

"That obvious?" I ask.

"Painfully."

My five fingers fit so well into hers. Like they were made for each other. I grip her hand, wanting to make sure she knows I'm not letting go. No way.

And when the cab finally pulls up to the address she gave, I still hold her hand even as I duck down and look outside.

What in the world?

She laughs. "Getting out? I have the fare."

"I can pay."

"This is my night."

42

The cab lets us out at a major intersection. Marvel leads me down a side street as if she's been here many times before.

"This reminds me of Lollapalooza."

"Except there's no music."

"There's music," Marvel says, and then I listen.

Sure enough, I can hear a song playing from the opened doors to a Mexican restaurant.

"Okay. But no band playing. And no crowds."

Marvel points at the people passing on the street.

"Do you always have to disagree?"

She shakes her head, then takes my hands in hers. I look at her and can't look away and I'm totally surprised.

What's she doing?

We begin to cross the street. Then she pulls me closer and I stand there for a moment, thinking she's joking, sure she's just playing around.

She's serious, you moron.

We're standing there on this street at night with dim lights and I move closer to her, then suddenly find myself kissing her. A sweet little kiss that she ends right away. But not in an awkward way or in an *enough already* sort of way. She simply moves back and gives me a happy, contented look. Like she's waited her whole life for this moment.

"Mar—"

That's all I can get out before a hand silences me.

She doesn't want me to ruin the moment, and goodness knows I will.

"Come on. I have something to show you."

She leads me down a street full of three- and four-story buildings, older with plenty of people hanging around them, inside and out. This must be some Latino section of the city. The street is alive with an energy I've never quite seen, not in the 'burbs.

"Here it is," she tells me.

She guides me through a wrought-iron gate with a broken lock. Then we walk down a very narrow alley until we get to a set of stairs—a fire escape. I follow her to the top of the four-story building.

When we reach the top, I hear music playing. It was in the background while we wandered up the stairs, but now it's clear.

The top is a wooden deck lined with stone walls and completely empty except for a doorway that leads to downstairs.

Marvel walks toward the edge of the building and leans over.

Below us is a brightly lit garden full of dancing couples and lively Mexican music and people eating and talking. It's a convergence of lawns behind four buildings. There are trees and flowers and a stone floor like a patio and tables all around. I can smell authentic Mexican food—the kind I've had at smaller dives in the suburbs. The meat cooking and all the spices and the hot sauces and the exotic flavors not found in pretty much *any* of Mom's dishes.

"What is this place?"

Marvel is looking down with a huge smile on her face. "Just watch."

The women are beautiful, much like Marvel. Dressed up in long-flowing dresses that seem to wave at me as they move on the dance floor. Men dressed up too, in suits and dress clothes and some even wearing cowboy hats and boots. I suddenly feel like I'm a different person, in a different place and time.

She locks an arm around mine as we watch.

Everyone sings along and cheers to a loud song that sounds like a celebration. After that there is a slow-moving song, sung in Spanish just like the last, where the women move passionately with the men.

I feel like I'm watching something special, some secret party, some magical moments. Such a different culture, especially because it seems like they're breaking out of the stiff boredom of life and having fun.

"How do you know this place?" I ask.

"I'll tell you later. Just let's watch."

So we do. Arm in arm, and then soon I'm beside her, then behind her with my arms around her.

"You've done this before, haven't you?"

She nods. I can not only see the smile on her face but can feel it on her skin and in her soul. It's breathing into mine and it's intoxicating.

It's only nine or so, and it looks like the party is just starting. Then I have an idea.

If it was just me, or me and Devon, or even me and Taryn or someone else, I'd never think this. But it's me and Marvel. *Marvella.*

"Have you ever been down there?"

"Where?"

"In the garden. In the party."

"No," she says. "Of course not."

"I think it's time," I say.

"I thought I was directing this night."

"I've never snuck up to the top of a Chicago high-rise and spied on an awesome party below. Nor have I ever been to a party like *that.*"

"Isn't it like something out of a movie?"

I nod. "Let's go down."

"No—what would we say?" she asks.

"You just ask them if we can join them to dance."

"*You* want to dance?"

I nod. "Yes. Down there? Yeah. Because that's not reality. This is some kind of dream, Marvel. This is heaven and I don't want to wake up. I want to dance with you down there. That's where you belong."

"Okay."

They play that perfect song. I've never heard it before and never will again, because I know they waited to play it for Marvel. The bells and the horns and the orchestra all play for us as we dance. Of course, who could tell this lovely Latina beauty no? With her floral skirt and cool vintage jacket and her hair up and pulled back. She fits in with them. Me? They don't even see me because she's so bright. They let us in with joy on their faces and in their hearts.

I want to move here. Tonight.

Marvel guides me as we dance. I don't really know what I'm doing and I really don't care. I laugh and feel drunk even though I haven't had anything. I don't *need* anything.

Hear that, Dad? I can get high on my own, thank you very much.

The lights surrounding us have a hypnotic aura about them. I honestly feel like I'm in some psychedelic dream. The moving figures are floating and bouncing and swaying.

I don't know how many songs we dance to. Two, three, maybe more.

Soon I feel her hand tugging at me, and she's leading me away from the main floor in the garden and back to the sidewalk and to the street.

"You don't want to stay?"

"I'm starving," she tells me.

"Oh, we're going to eat?"

I'm pretty hungry too, especially considering all the food that was surrounding us.

"I'm sure they would have let us stay and eat."

"I know," she says. "But I have somewhere else in mind."

Before we can go any further, I stop her. "Marvel—hold on."

"What?"

I'm sweaty and so is she. Her hair is messy, and I have to brush it away from her face. The cool breeze feels good.

"Is this real?" I ask.

"Of course."

We're on a tiny side street between garages and buildings and Dumpsters. I'm standing in a pothole. I can hear the main street nearby with cars honking and driving. It's not the most romantic place I've ever been. The place we just left—now *that* was romantic. Maybe I should wait for a better location, but I can't keep it in anymore.

"I love you."

Her mouth opens slightly in a surprised look. Not a bad surprise, but one that quickly turns into a full joyous pulling-down-the-moon-with-it sort of grin.

"I love you and I just can't keep it inside anymore," I tell her again. "I mean it. I do. I'm so crazy about you. From the moment I first saw you. It's just—it's all of me. Like every part."

She moves over and kisses me. Not some crazy passionate over-the-top kiss but a delicate one. Sweet and soft and perfect. Then she moves and still has that smile on her lips.

"I think I know this feeling you're talking about," she says.

Then she takes my hand and leads me by running down the back alleyway toward the street.

I can barely keep up with her.

43

Marvel takes me to a tiny hole-in-the wall restaurant with no sign on the front. The place is actually bigger than it looks from the outside, and it feels homey. Soft Mexican music plays and the smells are wonderful. A round woman brings us to a booth in the back where the lighting is low.

I quickly text my mom to tell her I'm hanging out with Devon and I'll be home later. This brief little message will surely make her not worry about anything. Especially since she's been more anxious ever since Artie Duncan's death at the beginning of summer.

"Was this one of your favorite places to come?" I ask after I put my phone away.

"My mother used to talk about this place. Said they had the best tacos in the city. She always talked about bringing Mirage and me, but we never got here."

"It's cool. I would've never thought this was a restaurant."

"It's almost hidden, which is why I think Mom liked it. Dad would've never been able to find it."

"Maybe nobody can find us tonight."

"I hope not," she says.

We order sodas, and then I ask her about the place we just left.

"Oh, yeah," she says. "Wasn't that just magical?"

"Do they have parties like that every night?"

"On the weekends they do. Even when it gets super cold."

"Did you used to live around there?"

"No. We had some friends there. Sometimes Mom and Dad would go to the party, and Mirage and I would watch from the bedroom we were supposed to be asleep in. That was when things were halfway normal in our house, when I was real young. I found a way to get to the top of the roof, and we'd go up there and watch for hours."

"But you didn't see your friends there tonight?"

"No, they moved away a long time ago. We stopped going. I wasn't sure if they still did the parties. But Mexicans love to get together for any sort of social event."

"I didn't want to leave."

"Me neither. But I did want to come here."

For the next hour it doesn't seem like I'm Brandon Jeffrey from Appleton, Illinois. And the young woman sitting across from me isn't Marvel Garcia. We are fugitives from a war we never started, and we've found ourselves safe now in this private haven that smells like salsa and fajitas. I forget our pasts and our age and our realities.

Tonight it's just Marvel and me.

Tonight there's no talk about her family except for good memories of her mother and Mirage. She doesn't talk about God's plan for her and the fact that she might die. The negative things remain far away, and that's where I like them to be.

We talk about silly things and fun things and the food and the music and I tell her how beautiful she is and how crazy I am about her and how I'd do anything she asked me to do.

"Careful saying things like that," Marvel says as she finishes a bite of her fish taco. "I might take you up on that."

"I mean it. I really do."

"Well, I have some ideas. But they're probably not the kind you might be thinking about."

"Guys all have the same one-track mind, huh?"

"You don't think like the other boys I've known."

"Have you ever been serious with anybody? Like with another guy?"

It's a subject we've never talked about.

"No. I was never like Taryn and you."

I groan. "Please don't open that wound. It's still an ugly little scab."

"I've made some mistakes. I just—I think because of my parents, and my father, and other things, I stayed away from guys. I was more concerned keeping my younger sister protected."

And just like that her eyes swell up with tears. It's that fast. Boom, she's got them and is wiping them away and taking in a deep breath.

"It comes and goes, anytime," Marvel says.

I reach over and take her hand. "I imagine it would."

"I'm okay, really."

She nods and forces a smile and composes herself. I finish the best burrito I've ever had in my life.

"This is really awesome."

"Tonight?"

I laugh. "No, I was talking about the food. But yeah, the night is too."

"You know, you're easy to be around."

"Well, you got used to that this summer."

"Some people get sick of being around each other, though. We always seem to barely get started. Talking and laughing and all that. It's pretty magical."

"Magical," I repeat. "That's the theme of this night. This sure beats graham crackers and cranberry juice."

"Hey—I don't know about that. That was magical in its own way."

"What if we saw Earl coming through those doors? Still with his beard half shaven?"

She laughs. "I'd let him sit right beside me, and I'd order him the fish tacos."

"Those were pretty awesome."

"I only let special people try my food. Hope you know that."

"Oh, I'm special. I've been told that all my life. Of course, when my family says it, it means something else."

"You are and will always be special, Brandon. I hope you know that. I hope you grow old realizing that."

I want to tell her the same thing but I don't. I don't because I don't want any sort of conversation about how that might not happen.

Maybe we'll be sitting here after our graduation day and we'll both realize we got through it. We survived *whatever.* We're both still here and still eating awesome Mexican food and still being special.

"I have one more idea in mind before we take the train home," she tells me.

"Can we skip the train?"

"I'd love to. But both of us would get in trouble."

"Yeah."

We take a cab to the lakefront, where we sit on a stone wall. It's cooler by the lake and forces us to bundle together and makes me want it to get even colder. In the distance we can see the lights extending out over the water on Navy Pier.

"We could've gone there," I tell her.

"I like this better. Less crowded. Less trendy."

"Heaven forbid Marvel Garcia ever becomes *trendy*."

"Shut up," she says, nudging me in the side.

The dark reflective surface of Lake Michigan hangs right in front of us. You can almost see all the stars on its surface. The water seems to reach forever. Sometimes it's hard to think of it only as a lake.

"I love standing next to something so immense," Marvel says. "It makes me think of 'How Great Thou Art' . . . 'I see the stars, I hear the rolling thunder, Thy power throughout the universe displayed.' My mother used to sing those old-time hymns."

My arm is around her while we look out toward the dark and feel the night air breathing against us. I don't say anything. I just let her keep talking and sharing her thoughts.

"Sometimes it's a nice reminder of how small we are compared to the vastness of God and his creation. Our problems can look so tiny when you look at it that way. When you realize our time here—even if we live to be a hundred—is just one tiny little blink."

"Sometimes it feels very, very long," I say. "Like in my calculus class."

She laughs. "Yeah. Sometimes I can hear the minutes stuck on the clock when I'm at my uncle and aunt's apartment. I can't wait to get out of there."

"Just another year or so," I tell her.

You mentioned time. Don't mention time.

"Yeah," she says, her voice trailing off.

I move my head so I can face her. Then I give her a long kiss.

"Kisses like that don't feel tiny," I tell her when I move away. "I wish I could make them last a very long time."

"Okay," she says, kissing me again.

44

Why can't kisses last, and the emotions felt during them stay?
Eventually they're over, and the emptiness creeps back in. I'd
love to have that full feeling inside of me all the time. I'd love
to have it inside my heart morning, noon, and night.

Later that night, after holding Marvel in the cab ride and
then on the train and even on the drive back to her apartment, I find myself in my own bed. Sleep is hard but it eventually comes.

It brings some strange friends with it.

The first person I see clearly in my dream is Marvel's uncle,
Carlos. He is looking over me and smiling. His fist is bloody,
and then I realize I can taste it in my mouth. I'm sore. No,
I'm not just sore. I think my face is broken. Then I look
on the ground and see Seth looking scared and choking
up blood.

Then things go really, really wacky.

I see this white puddle with red drops in it. I realize it's milk and it's got blood splattered in it. Then a boot print splashes it everywhere.

I hear screams and look up to see if Carlos is doing something, but he's gone. So is Seth. The scream is coming from beneath me.

I search, but it's cloudy and I can't see. I call out to the screaming person.

Then I hear thunder and it makes me fall on my knees.

The sound of someone singing "How Great Thou Art" plays on speakers above my head.

I feel myself moving, running, sucking in air. Then I strike a wall, feeling the flat brick bursting against my face and my gut. I can't move. I'm stuck.

Yet the screams follow me. They're behind me now, and louder. I turn and somehow I manage to fall out of my bed.

Man, I need to lighten up the mood just a bit.

Seeing Marvel makes me want to rush up and grab her and swing her around like those dancers we watched. We're back in the familiar hallways of Appleton High, but I don't loathe being here. I love it. I love knowing she's there and I can, if I want, make it become a high school musical for a moment and make the most of seeing her this morning.

"Hey," is what I actually say, instead of picking her up and twirling her around.

She gives me a kiss on the cheek, then mimics my laid-back greeting.

"How's life?"

"*Life* is good," Marvel says. "Every day is a gift, right?"

I nod. "With you around it sure is."

"Aww. That's the best answer you could possibly give."

"It's the only one that came to mind."

She takes my hand and we walk to class. Gone are the nightmares that follow me in my sleep or occasionally find me in these classrooms.

The first brush with reality comes when Devon shows me another text.

"This is from the same guy who asked if I needed anything since Artie was gone. Then later sent me a message saying to come alone next time."

"Did you ever respond?" I ask.

Devon nods. "Yeah. I asked when and where. But nothing. Until now."

I look at his phone.

No surprises. This Friday night. Meet at quarry.

I sigh. Then I think of who this might possibly be coming from.

Jeremy Simmons.

I think of the fight club and the hard-core dudes Jeremy was hanging around with.

"I don't think you should go."

"I already said yes," he says.

"Then why are you showing me?"

"I don't know. In case something happens."

"In case something *happens*? Devon, that's not even funny." I want to hit the guy over the head.

"I'm not being funny."

"A guy died."

"I know."

"You have no idea what kind of person this is."

"Probably some stoner."

Jeremy's not a stoner dude.

"So what—you're going to buy, and then what?"

"Then see what happens. Develop a relationship."

"It's a bad idea. Period. Seriously. You shouldn't do it."

"I'm doing it. Frankie gets to be a hero on the football field and you get to date the pretty new girl, but what about me?"

"*This* is no way to be a hero. This is being stupid."

"Like you haven't done any stupid things in your life."

I know that this is hopeless.

"I'm not saying I've never done stupid things. I have. All the time. But don't you want me to tell you if I think you're being an idiot?"

"Yeah, I guess," Devon says.

"Okay, you're being an idiot."

"Just—just be around on Friday, okay?"

"Oh, sure. You want me to be 'backup' to something I think is a stupid idea in the first place."

We have to go to class before we reach any sort of resolution, and soon I mostly forget about it.

Until late Friday night when I get a call from Devon. A very bad call.

45

"Brandon, you gotta come out here and help me."

It's Devon. He's breathless and serious. It's 11:34 p.m., so it can't be anything good.

"What happened?"

"I'll tell you when you get here."

"I'm not going anywhere. Have you been jogging or something?"

"I need your help."

"With what?"

He pauses, then, still breathless, says, "Marvel's uncle."

I think anything he might have said would have sounded better. Suddenly I get this lump in my gut and wonder why in the world Devon has anything to do with Marvel's uncle. I'm no longer annoyed. Now I'm curious and desperate to know what's going on.

"Where are you?"

"The quarry. I'm in the parking lot."

"You okay?"

He's panting now. "No. Yeah. I'm fine, but I don't know. Just come."

"Should I call the cops?"

He curses. "No. No. I got—no, just get out here fast. And make sure you're not followed."

My headlights cutting through the empty black of the parking lot eventually find Devon's Jeep and Devon standing right beside it. I pull up beside him and roll down my window.

"What's up?"

"Were you followed?"

"Yeah. A couple of unmarked vans just on the horizon. No."

He looks down the road I just came from.

"What's happening? What's the deal with Marvel's uncle?"

"I went to buy the pot tonight. From that guy. The house we were at?"

"You went back there?"

Devon shakes his head. "No. He met me in the parking lot of a Taco Bell."

I roll my eyes. "Did he order you a chalupa too?"

Devon curses at me. "This is serious."

"So what happened?"

"Everything went fine. This guy—Jeremy something."

"You met Jeremy Simmons?"

He nods. "Man, that guy's scary."

You don't know the half of it.

"So what happened?"

"I got the pot and then drove back home, but someone was following me. I get a bit freaked, thinking it's a cop or something, but he's driving this black Trans Am so I'm thinking it's not. I don't know. So I drive around and around and then he nearly runs me off the road."

The sinking feeling in my stomach is back.

"I drove into a park, and that's when he blocked me off and got out of the car. I recognized him—Marvel's uncle. I've seen him picking her up at school."

I think of all the afternoons I can't drive her back to her apartment, and I suddenly wish I didn't have soccer practice. I'd quit the team just to have more time with her. *And* to keep her away from her uncle.

"He looks like he's about to pull me through the window and he says to give him the pot, so I just—I was afraid."

"So what'd you do?"

"Shh, don't talk so loud," he says.

So I whisper it again.

There's a quiet and creepy stillness over the quarry that freaks me out. I can't help it; this place at night has always given me the creeps.

"I pulled a gun on him and told him to back off."

I wait for him to say, "Just kidding," but he doesn't.

"Shut up."

"I did."

"What are you doing with a gun?"

I'm sort of yelling/whispering. It'd be funny if I weren't so freaked out that it's Marvel's uncle we're talking about.

"I got it a month ago."

"How?"

"My parents bought it for me. It's licensed to them. They let me keep it in my room."

Are they high? Oh, wait, it's Devon's parents.

"What kind of gun?"

"It's a Glock. Cool little gun."

"Oh, as opposed to your *bigger* guns?" I ask.

"Shut up."

"So then you just what—drove off?"

He nods.

"Did he follow you?"

"No. But he didn't look too happy when I left."

"Carlos," I say, as if I get together with him on a regular basis.

"Yeah. He looked . . . dangerous."

"Maybe because you shoved a *Glock* in his face."

"He was trying to steal my drugs."

I shake my head. "You're an idiot. Seriously. I told you not to go. You shouldn't be messing with these people, Devon. You're no Walter White."

"Maybe it's my time to 'break bad.'"

"No. You're not breaking bad. You're not breaking a bit. You're . . ."

I don't have the words to adequately tell him how stupid he happens to be.

"So why'd you call me? What do you expect me to do?"

He shakes his head. "I don't know. I just—I'm scared to go home."

46

I breathe in, thinking again about what I'm doing—
skipping out of school for half an hour—and what I'm
about to do—confront Carlos. Across the street from where
I parked is the body shop where Marvel told me her uncle
works. Next to me on the seat is a paper lunch bag, its top
folded nice and neat.

You still can go back to school. You can still stay out of this.

But there's no way I'm out of this. Absolutely no way.

I get out of the SUV and walk across the street. I open the
door to the body shop, and a balding man sitting at a messy
desk looks up.

"Can I help you?"

"I'm looking for Carlos," I say.

The paper bag is in my right hand.

The guy nods and puts down his pen. He heads to the
back of the shop, which looks like a big garage. In a minute
I see Carlos, wearing the same kind of shirt as the bald guy
and giving me a completely grim look. He doesn't even wait

for me to say something; he just walks past me and exits the shop. I follow.

When we get outside he looks at me as if he's debating whether to smash my face in or punch me in the gut.

"What do you want?"

I shove the bag into his hands, forcing him to take it. He doesn't look down, but continues glaring at me.

"This is what you tried to take from my friend last night. Here. It's yours. He's an idiot and doesn't mean to be messing with anybody."

Now Carlos glances down at the bag, then back at me. He laughs.

"Leave Devon alone," I say.

"You come to *my* work to give me *this*?" He curses in Spanish.

"You came to my work, so I thought I'd return the favor."

He laughs. "You got a lot of guts," Carlos tells me. "And I admire that, even if I think you're the dumbest kid I've ever seen. Dumber than your friend. You bring a gun too?"

I shake my head.

"You don't know what you're doing, kid," he says. "The wrong people and the wrong place and the wrong everything. That's you."

"My friend isn't going to be bothering you anymore."

Carlos smiles. "You don't get it. You can't even *begin* to get it."

He turns around and looks into the shop, then back at me.

"You know—it's not like I have no idea you're hanging out with Marvel," Carlos says. "You think I'm dumb or something? But I told you I didn't want to see you. I didn't want any trace of you in my life. Yet here you are."

I don't say anything because there's nothing I can say. I feel like water that's about ready to be poured out of a cup into the sink. But I stay steady. That's all I can do.

"You're way more stupid than I thought," he tells me. "But that's okay. In time, Brandon. In time."

"Leave me and my friend alone," I say.

"You'd better get a gun too," he whispers to me. "'Cause you're gonna need one. I promise you that."

He heads back into the shop, carrying the bag.

As far as I'm concerned, we're square and that's the end of the story.

That's what I'll tell Devon and what I'll act like when it comes to Marvel.

That's what I'll tell myself, too. I just hope I end up believing it.

47

It's a weeknight in late October and I'm "working" at the record store, bored out of my mind. It's more like babysitting a property than working at a retail store. I'd hate to have to try to be a musician these days. Or worse, someone who has to make a living selling music.

The only person who has come in all evening is Lee Fleisher, a regular who comes in once a week to look around. He's an older guy with round cheeks and a rounder neck who loves his tropical shirts and flip-flops regardless of the weather. We talk awhile, and he asks about Marvel and Harry. Then, as he's checking out, buying an album I've never heard of, he asks if I'm looking for some more work.

"Yeah, actually, a little more work would be great," I tell him. "Now that I don't cut grass anymore."

"You pretty good with your money?" he asks.

"I save it, yeah. I don't spend a lot."

"That's good. I'd love to have some help in the yard. I need the leaves raked—kid who used to do it for me went away to college. I hate those professional landscaping companies who just keep bothering you even when you have nothing for them to do."

"Yeah, anything I can do."

He gives me a card. "This is for my business, even though I'm retired now. But the number is still good. Call me sometime."

I thank him and wish him a good night. I can always use extra money for college, even if I have no idea where I'm going. A little in the bank is a good thing.

I'm assuming nobody else is going to come in tonight, so when I hear the door chime I turn around expecting to see Marvel. I'd bet a hundred bucks on it. Instead I see Seth Belcher, his expression typically indifferent.

"Hey, man," I call out.

I don't even have any music playing, an oversight that Harry would frown on.

Seth walks up to the desk.

"You guys don't sell graphic novels, do you?" he asks.

"No. Maybe sometime. Harry's asked about them every now and then."

"You should get some," Seth says, looking behind me at the various collectibles and high-priced items behind the glass counter.

"What brings you in here?"

He shrugs and keeps looking around, but it's obvious he's got something on his mind. So I make small talk for a while, which is mostly one-sided. He's got such an awkward way about him that it's difficult to say anything without feeling stupid. But I keep trying, thinking I'm making him feel more comfortable.

Eventually, however, he asks me the question I think he came in with.

"What made you come over and get involved when Greg and Sergio were fighting with me?"

I think of that first time I saw him, on the ground in the bike park. It didn't look like he was "fighting with" them. It looked like he was getting his butt kicked in.

"Seemed like you needed a little help."

"You don't like Greg, do you?"

I shake my head.

"You hear about his car getting spray-painted?"

I smile. "Yeah."

Seth looks at me. "You know he blames me?"

"Really? He try to do anything to you?"

Seth shakes his head, not seeming too worried about it. "You know anything about it?"

"Nope," I lie.

I'm not about to tell Seth the truth. Especially in the event that Greg and his buddies try to do something to him. Seth will surely blame me.

It was harmless anyway. The paint all came off.

"You ever think about doing something really nasty to Greg?"

Something about the way he says *nasty* is kinda creepy. I shake my head.

"You sure? 'Cause you know—I have some ideas."

I think of Seth's buddy, Jeremy, and the weird fight club in the barn.

"I want to stay out of things."

"Oh, is that what you're doing?" Seth says.

He knows. He knows I did it.

"Yep, that's what I'm doing." I just give him a nice, happy grin.

"Tell me . . . do you think Greg has ever been scared of something? Like really scared? Like waking up in the middle of the night barely able to breathe sort of scared?"

"I doubt it."

Seth nods, then smiles and murmurs, "Hmm."

"Why?"

"I have a nice imagination," he says.

And with that, he leaves. As he's walking out the door, I call good-bye, but I'm not sure if he hears me.

What an odd duck. That's all I gotta say.

That night I hear shoveling in my dreams. I can see dirt being dug up and hoisted over to the side, though I'm not the one doing it. It's late night, because it's dark and quiet.

Someone's coughing, spitting up, choking almost.

The hole being dug is big. And deep. Several feet deep. Deep enough to put someone in.

Wake up—this isn't going to end well.

Then the coughing and spitting stops. I hear a groan, then a slight yell, then a heavy thud. Then the coughing continues.

The scene runs like a movie, as all my dreams have been doing lately.

What is wrong with me?

"No please, no please."

The words are barely audible, but I know who's saying them. I want to bend down and help the figure in the hole now. I try to scream, but nothing comes out. I want to run but can't. I want to move but I'm stuck. I want to do anything. Anything.

"Help," the gasping voice says.

It's Devon.

He's the one in the hole.

He's the one coughing up something dark.

The digging starts again.

No.

The dirt is falling on top of the body.

No. No. He's still alive.

More. Over. Over.

Please stop, please let me wake up.

I have to listen and watch as the dirt fills the hole and the coughing gets covered up and then I hear gasping and choking and screaming, but nobody comes.

I can't do a single thing about it.

The next morning, feeling groggy and hungover and wondering why I'm losing my mind, I send Devon a quick text.

Hey what's up?

Anything else and he'll wonder if I'm crazy.

Nothing. About to head to school. You sick?

I let out a sigh of relief. I know it was crazy to worry, but I couldn't help it.

Yeah, sick of school, I write. **I'll see you soon.**

He gives me a smiley face on the phone. I can't help remembering those sickly coughs as he was buried alive in my dreams.

I think about his gun. Devon's Glock. The one he pointed at Carlos.

Maybe I should tell him to carry it around with him. In case someone digs a hole for him.

Maybe I should also ask if he has another. I definitely might end up needing it.

48

That Friday, a week before Halloween, starts with tears. I see them on Marvel's face as I pull up to her apartment. I don't even wait for her to climb inside the Honda. I put the SUV in park and then I'm out, rounding the vehicle and holding her to make sure she's okay.

"What's wrong?"

"Let's get in the car."

"Are you okay?"

She nods and wipes her cheeks. I open the door for her, then before I get in, I look back at the building. I check to see if anybody is watching us, maybe by the entryway or through a window. But I don't see anybody. Nor do I see anybody in the parking lot who looks familiar.

"So tell me, what's wrong?" I ask her as we head to school.

She swallows, wiping her eyes, cringing a bit.

"Marvel?"

"It's my uncle. It's been—things have been bad lately. And he just . . ."

She loses control again. I pull off to the side of the road and park the car. Then I take her hand and ask her to tell me.

"He's acting like my father did," Marvel says. "And I just— I get this feeling. I'm scared. I just feel the evil inside of him."

"It's okay," I tell her. "It's going to be okay."

"I see the way he looks at me. It's wrong, Brandon. I don't have to wonder what that look means. I know, and it terrifies me. I couldn't sleep at all last night. I'm afraid to be in there."

I think for a second about telling her about her uncle and everything that's happened recently. But another voice deep down inside shuts that idea up right away.

"We have to tell someone," I say instead.

There's always something you can do. Whether it's necessarily a *good* idea, well . . .

"There's nothing to tell," she says. "He hasn't done anything."

"But he might. You need to tell someone. A teacher or guidance counselor or cop or somebody."

"I can't."

"You have to," I tell her. "Or else come stay with me."

"My uncle hates my aunt, and she hates me. It's like she blames me. And . . . and I don't know. Maybe she should. Maybe everybody's right."

She begins to cry again.

"What?"

"Maybe they're all right."

"Who's right?" I ask. "What are you talking about?"

"The comments online. People saying I brought this evil to Appleton. Talking about my dead family. I know. I've seen them."

I curse. "I wanted to kill Taryn for doing that."

"It doesn't matter."

"Yes it does," I say, enraged all over again by what Taryn did.

"There is an evil here. In this town. In my uncle. Brandon—something is happening. I don't know what, but I'm scared."

"It's okay," I tell her, holding her and looking at her.

"You don't understand."

I understand more than she knows.

"I love you," I say.

"I know you do."

"Nothing is going to happen to you."

"I'm scared for others, too. For you. For your friends. For the innocent."

"Don't let your uncle freak you out."

"I found a verse this morning," she says, her body starting to shake, her eyes still watery. "It says, 'I have given you authority over all the power of the enemy, and you can walk among snakes and scorpions and crush them. Nothing will injure you.'"

"Then remember that, okay?"

I'm just trying to encourage her.

"I know who the enemy is, and I know that God is in control, but I'm scared. I'm just so . . ."

She weeps in my chest. Like a waterfall of emotion and sadness and fear that I can't do a thing about. So I just hold her. I don't even tell her it's going to be okay, because I don't know if it is. I really don't.

I feel myself shaking now. I blink away tears from my eyes. All of a sudden I think of something and it's awful and it's right.

Devon's gun.

I think of this. Then I think of Marvel's uncle. What he said. The way I fully believed he meant it.

I know it's an awful idea. I know the very idea of confronting her uncle is just not good. But holding her and seeing her like this and thinking something might happen, something bad, something maybe even worse than death . . .

"Nothing will injure you, okay?" I tell her.

It might actually be the first time in my life I've used a Bible verse in a sentence. But I mean it.

I intend to be her guardian angel. A really messy and flawed one, but that's okay. I can get the job done.

A little later that morning, before having the necessary conversation with Devon, I end up imagining it in my head.

"Hey, I need to ask you something."

"Look who's being all secretive now."

"Shut up and listen. I need to borrow your gun."

"Now?"

I can hear Devon asking me *why* and asking me *when*, but I can see eventually wearing him down.

"But isn't the whole point to protect people?" another voice asks. This one sounds a lot like someone like Harry. *"When guns show up, people end up getting hurt."*

"Is this an anti-gun ad?" I reply in my imaginary conversation.

"You have a psycho for a father, and Carlos is making threats against you, and you want to add a gun to that *mix?"*

It's a reasonable point. So I decide to not ask Devon for his Glock.

Not just yet.

But I know it's there, and somehow that's comforting.

49

Marvel doesn't want to get together tonight, but she says I shouldn't worry about her because her uncle is working late. I try to persuade her, but she won't budge. So I hang out with the guys at Devon's house and watch a movie, play some games, act like life is somewhat normal.

When I get home I go online and check Marvel's Facebook page, then I go to see if she blogged any more. There's a new entry she just posted.

A HAND ALONG THE STUMBLE

Maybe you wait to hear His voice
So what happens when He breaks the noise?
What happens when the heavens open up
Only to tell you everything you don't want to know?
Maybe the spirit is weak
Maybe the spirit stubborn
Maybe the soul is tired

Maybe it's just time
I believe I believe and I believe more
I care and I love
But I want to take a breath before I fall
I want to smile before I cry
Is it wrong even though you're doing His will?
Is it bad to hold a hand as you stumble over the falls?
I need relief
I need some quiet comfort
Swollen with grief
Even though I'm still here
I choose this time
Because time is something I don't have
I choose this hand
Because one day I know I'll have to let go

I let out a sigh and close my eyes, feeling heavier than I did a moment before.

"Before I fall" and "stumble over the falls" and "I'll have to let go"?

Every day it seems like Marvel is telling herself that it's her time to go.

But go where? Why? What for?

I keep trying to think of the where and why and what for.

The thing with Artie Duncan . . . it's just a really awful thing that happened and has nothing to do with Marvel.

Devon and his whole drug-dealing weird conspiracy theory? I don't know.

Seth and his weirdo friends? They're just strange.

Marvel's uncle? Well, yeah, maybe.

I keep trying to figure it out, but I'm getting nowhere.

"I'm still here."

Yes, Marvel. Yes you are.

I keep thinking of Devon's gun. Of how I'm going to handle her uncle. Well, I should really say how I'm going to react the moment he shows up. It's in the same hellish category as my father. A nightmare waiting to be stepped into at any given moment.

But that's *my* nightmare.

I'm hoping that Marvel isn't going to have to endure another one. God knows she's had enough in her life already.

So whatever it takes and whatever I have to do and whatever nightmare I need to step into, so be it.

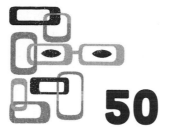

50

I see it in the parking lot of the apartment buildings: Carlos's black Pontiac Firebird Trans Am. I've been sitting here in my car for almost an hour now. Waiting to see when he gets in and where he'll go. I fully intend to follow.

I'm ready.

Marvel texted me that her uncle was working at his second job tonight. I want to see where that second job happens to be. I recall the night Devon and I were spying on the warehouse with the smokestack and I saw Carlos drive by. Now I think it wasn't a coincidence after all.

I've thought of something else. Another way to get a gun.

I bet if I asked Jeremy Simmons, or maybe went through Seth to ask him, I could get my hands on one.

I've never pointed a gun at anybody. I've never even threatened anyone. Not the way they do in movies, the life-or-death sort of threat. But I'm ready. I can imagine owning a gun and one day aiming it at Carlos if I have to. Telling

him that if anything happens to Marvel I'll come back for
him.

Yeah, maybe it could be that easy. Maybe I could do that.

*Yeah, and maybe you can score three goals in a single game.
Yeah right.*

A tapping sound makes me jump. Thankfully I'm not
holding a gun in my hand. It might have gone off. I turn,
expecting to see Carlos, but the figure standing outside my
window is one I know quite well.

"Hey, Phil," I say when I roll down my window.

"Do you mind taking me back home?"

Where did he come from? It's dark in this parking lot,
and he seemed to emerge from the shadows.

"What are you doing here?" I ask.

"Oh, just staying out of trouble. How 'bout you?"

Something about the way he says this makes me laugh.
It's still in his Phil-talk sort of way. Relaxed, with a yeah-
man-peace-out-dude feel. But it's also got a bit of an edge
to it.

"I was just, uh, waiting for someone."

"Cool," he says. "Here I am."

"Well, yeah. Here you are."

"So what do you say? Can you take me home?"

"I don't know. I mean—right now isn't the best time."

"Sure it is. I mean—you might get in trouble waiting
around in a parking lot for someone. Or worse yet, following
them in your car."

I look at Phil and think my mouth is hanging wide open.

"What . . ."

"Take me home, Brandon."

This isn't a request anymore.

"Okay."

I drive toward downtown Appleton while I try to figure out how in the world Phil knows I was waiting there for Marvel's uncle. I can't remember ever talking to him about Marvel, much less Carlos.

"How'd you know I was—"

"Don't worry about how I know," he interrupts.

"What do you think I was doing?"

He only smiles, then he rubs his beard and looks out the window at the sleeping town of Appleton.

"Want to know the best thing about getting old? People don't pay much attention to you. But you can pay *lots* of attention to them."

"Like spying?"

"I'm just trying to help you out, Brandon."

"But why—what do you mean?"

"Sometimes you have to be patient and trust that God has a plan."

Here we go again with the God's plan thing. Everybody seems to know God's got a plan.

"I wasn't going to do anything," I tell him.

"Keep going straight," Phil says.

"This is freaking me out a bit."

"Really?"

I nod.

"Don't let it," Phil says in a matter-of-fact way. "Just let things be. Okay?"

I look at him, a scrawny guy who is probably a whole lot stronger than his physique suggests. He could have a gun or a knife on him and be leading me out to carve me up.

"And don't look at me that way. I'm not a bad guy."

"How am I supposed to know?"

"You know. You let me in the car, right?"

There's always been *something* about Phil. The very first time I met him, he shook my hand and then got a strange look on his face. Like a light went on, or a bell went off in his mind. Like he'd met me before or something. And ever since then, I've caught him looking at me from time to time. Observing me a little more.

"Turn left at the stoplight," he says.

"How'd you get over to the apartments?" I ask.

"Man, you're sure not this inquisitive at the record store."

"It just seems weird."

"Lemme tell you something, okay? I saved you a whole world of hurt tonight. Because something told me you were about to do something *stupid*. When you're young and sixteen, you can be stupid. I was stupid."

"I'm seventeen."

"Well, that makes you even *more* stupid, because you're a year older."

"How did you know I was there?"

"Stop asking questions and start trying to hear the answers," Phil says. "That girl's uncle? He's one of the bad ones. A bad egg, as they say. You should not in any way be messin' around with him, you got that?"

"What if he hurts Marvel?"

"I understand. But some things are out of your control."

"How do you know about all of this? Did you talk to Devon?"

I can't help asking these questions.

"Turn up there—the second street. That's mine."

I turn, and he directs me to a small, one-story house. I park at the curb in front, but Phil doesn't get out of the car right away.

For a moment he looks through the front windshield as if he's thinking long and hard about something.

"So here's the deal, Brandon. Some bad things have come our way. I've been waiting, and I knew—I knew the moment I heard about the poor boy being gutted up—I knew."

"What do you mean, 'bad things'?"

"I mean a war happening right here. Good versus evil. Light versus darkness."

"Did Marvel's uncle have anything to do with Artie's death?"

Phil shakes his head. "I don't know. Maybe or maybe not. But that's just the start. I know this. I've known about it for a long time. And listen. I don't know—I'm not sure why—but I know that girl, Marvel, she's someone special."

"I know. Why do you think I'm trying to help her out?"

"This is a lot bigger than just about a boy having a crush on a girl."

The way he says that irritates me. No, it doesn't just irritate me. It makes me feel really stupid and young and naive.

"You ever loved someone?"

"Of course I have. I know. I understand what's there." He taps my chest. "I know what's pulsing through that heart of yours and that head. But we boys—and all of us can be boys when we want to be—can do dumb, dumb things."

"What are you talking about—a war?"

"I know there are things you don't understand and don't believe, Brandon. But I pray that you will. And I pray that this darkness doesn't grow. I pray for all of us. For this town. For the people in it."

If this is supposed to be some kind of cool pep talk, Phil sure is missing the mark.

"Listen to me. You got a lot going on. You don't need to add more bad men to your life. You got that? For now, Marvel's uncle stays away from you. Keep it that way."

"How do you know about—"

"I just know," he says in a voice loud enough to shut me up. "I just know."

With that he gives me a nod, opens the door, and heads out into the darkness.

51

A couple of nights before Halloween, the devil decides to pay an early visit to our house to trick-or-treat. Except he's not standing on the doorstep. And he's not asking for a treat. He's come to play his evil tricks since he's currently out-of-his-mind drunk and the house is quiet.

It's late, and I'm watching a movie. I assumed that Mom and Dad were upstairs asleep and that Alex and Carter were either asleep or playing video games in the game room. When my dad suddenly shows up in the family room, I almost jump.

He curses at me, then shakes his head. "Do you ever—*ever*—do a single thing I ask you to do?"

I sit up on the couch. "Yes, sir."

"What'd I tell you about that little Mexican girl you've been hanging around with? Huh? What'd I tell you?"

I heard your words loud and clear, you miserable drunk. I just disobeyed them.

He walks closer to the couch.

"If I wasn't under lock and key I'd drag your lazy butt off

that couch and down the driveway and toss you out into the street. That's what I'd do. And I'd stomp that smug little face of yours. You know that?"

He grits his teeth, and I can just feel the rage. It's like a piping hot blanket coming over me, burning me, smothering me.

"But once I'm no longer being *monitored*, boy, I'm gonna have some fun. You and me are gonna finish some business. You got that?"

I can't help but grit my teeth too. I'm not cowering and I'm not backing down.

"Look at you, you little weasel. Think you're so tough, don't you?" Dad spits on the floor as if we're outside on a football field.

I keep my mouth shut.

"Got nothing, huh? I figured you didn't. But I'm waiting. I'm waiting, you got that?" He grabs my hair and speaks through clenched teeth. "Do? You? Get? That?"

I feel like a clump of my hair is going to tear off my head. "Yes, sir."

Some people use curse words. I use *yessirs*.

He lets go of me, and his eyes close. I think he's going to pass out right there and collapse in my lap. But then he opens them again, turns around, and walks out of the room.

I hear Phil's words again.

You listen to me. You got a lot going on. You don't need to add more bad men to your life. You got that?

Phil is right. I need fewer bad men in my life.

Maybe I need a good gun to make life a little better.

Don't be a moron and don't even pretend to think something like that.

Suddenly the movie I'm watching isn't quite as dramatic as the life I'm living. I decide to head to my room and lock the door and then contact Marvel.

I need a little hope and encouragement tonight.

I hate my father.

I wait a long time before Marvel texts me back.

The world has enough hate in it. Don't hate him.

The monster came back tonight, I write.

You okay? He hit you?

No. But he's going to. Any day now.

I'm sorry.

Are you okay? I ask.

Yes.

Remember our pact, okay? If one of us is hurt . . .

I'm sorry you're hurt tonight, Marvel writes.

Yeah.

If I could take it away, I would.

Yeah.

Someone else has, you know.

I don't say yeah this time. Most of the time when she starts with her Jesus talk, I go along. But I don't want to. Not tonight.

Not trying to be glib. I mean that.

I know. I just don't accept it. That God's Son said, yeah, I'm going to die for you. No. Too much for me to believe.

I know. I'm not trying to force you to believe. When the time is right you will.

I read that last sentence several times.

What if there never is a "right" time? You sound confident.

I hope. That's better to do than hate.

I want to kill him.

There's another long pause.

Do you think I didn't feel the same way about my father?

He's no longer there, I write.

I could still hate him, you know. But I choose love. I choose to forgive. I have to choose that every day because I want to hate him.

Why can fathers be such monsters?

My heavenly Father isn't. That's what I keep going back to. He loves me the way I should be loved. I know that. I believe that.

What am I supposed to do with that? Sometimes she makes me want to toss my phone.

Brandon, listen—I see you. And I'm not the only one. You need to know something. Please.

What?

It's important you carry the certainty of being loved with you. Now. And all of your life.

Once again, this girl leaves me speechless. Breathless, in fact. I'm bleeding, and she comes and stitches up the wound. She doesn't preach at me; she just shares what she believes, knowing I'm not on the same page.

But I so want that sort of hope and happiness she has. I want it. I need it.

Thank you.

I love you, Brandon.

I force myself not to cry. Good tears, bad tears, scared tears, wonderful tears.

No, I won't—I can't, come on.

But I'm wiping them away.

I love you too, Marvel. More than I can possibly tell you or show you.

Stay safe. I'm praying for peace. For both of our hearts. And our messy homes.

Amen, I text. **See you tomorrow.**

It can't come fast enough.

52

Fascination Street Records feels like more of a home to Marvel and me than the actual houses we go to every night. It's the evening before Halloween, and we're both "working" even though we weren't supposed to come in and Harry's not paying us. But he told us "lovebirds" to close down the store when we're finished. It's going to be a big night here tomorrow with a book signing with local horror writer Dennis Shore, so Harry's left early.

At ten o'clock the store lights are still on. It's been a fun evening spent laughing and playing music and cleaning up and talking about anything and everything. I just like hiding out in this place. The world doesn't bother us, and that's a great thing.

"Come to the party Halloween night," I ask her again.

"I'd rather stay here and serve all the customers."

"We haven't had a customer all night."

She smiles.

"Come on."

"Why are you going?"

"My buddies."

"And girls dressed up in slutty costumes."

"That's not why I'm going."

"Or maybe you just want to see Taryn's parents."

Yeah, the party is at Taryn's house. That means it's going to be big and outrageous.

"That's why I was considering not going."

She shakes her head. "Don't worry. I'm not jealous."

"You should be."

"It's just—I think it's wrong glorifying some holiday that celebrates the darkness."

I nod. "Okay. Well, I'm not dressing up."

"No?"

"No. All my slutty outfits are on loan to Devon."

"Please. I'll never get that image out of my mind."

Before the night is over I make sure to tell her something I've been thinking ever since texting with her last night.

"Thank you. For being there."

"Sure," she says.

"It means a lot. It means everything."

"I'm glad I can say something."

I wrap my arms around her and kiss her. In the background, the new band London Grammar sings to us about life and love and other things. It's a really nice moment.

No. It's perfect.

As we walk to my car I watch her looking up at the stars and seeming so carefree.

"So there you go."

"What?" she asks.

"You're there and you're just—you're content. You're okay. You walk and you look up and seem in wonder of what you're looking at. The sky. Or the stars. Or whatever. And all I'm doing is wondering who you are. Wondering what you're talking about. Wondering if there's a God or heaven up there."

She nods.

"I'm sorry," I say.

"It's okay."

"No it's not. Marvel, I want to believe."

"You can."

"But I just . . ."

I've never really identified the true question swirling around inside my head. Or the exact wondering in my soul.

I guess I want to say that if God does exist, then why could he allow these bad things to happen?

Why would he allow me to have such a failure of a father? *That's* what I want to know. *That's* what I'm wondering about.

Marvel takes my hand.

"I can't force you to believe anything," she tells me. "I'm not trying to do anything except love you."

I look at her and can't say anything.

It's one thing to read it in a text, but hearing her say it out loud, in person . . .

"That's right, Brandon. I love you. In my own weird little way."

I shake my head. It's too much. She's too much, and that's exactly why I need her in my life and can't let her go.

"You make me believe that I could just scoop up all those stars above us and hold them in my hands," I say. "You know that?"

"And you say you're not a romantic." She glows. Her face, her smile, her everything.

"But Marvel . . . what in the world would I do with the stars in my hands?"

She grips my hand.

"Come on."

"What—where are we going?" I ask.

"Just up ahead. It's not far."

"And then?"

"We'll just have to wait. And believe."

She smiles. I can believe there's a God when I look at a beautiful face like that. A smile like Marvel's.

So I walk alongside her. Full of questions. But feeling like she's carrying some of them.

It feels good.

That'd be a cool way to end a story, right? This is how I'd end it, hand in hand, feeling good, having some hope, eyes stretching toward belief, walking down a sidewalk to head to the river to just hold each other and gaze at the stars.

Hope finding its way into my heart. And the very idea and possibility of believing in this God Marvel talks about becoming a real, true thing.

This is how the story should end.

53

Halloween arrives, however, and its dark night seems to have other plans.

Everything about the day seems overcast, starting with the skies that cloud over and then progressively get worse with storms coming. Something is off with Marvel's mood at school, and Devon seems nervous for some reason. Kids are behaving like idiots, ready for Friday night trick-or-treating and partying and misbehaving.

I drop by the record store for a while to help with the book signing. Big-name scary writer Dennis Shore has a new book coming out, a horror novel about a man falling in love with a ghost. It's called *Shine On You Crazy Diamond*, which Harry tells me continues the author's use of Pink Floyd songs as titles. All night the record store is blasting Pink Floyd. The store is crowded with tons of people. I've never seen it this packed.

Marvel says she's going to come by but she doesn't, so I decide to head out to see her before going over to Devon's to ride with him and other guys to the party. Harry's wife, Sarah, is here tonight helping, along with Phil, so they've got enough people.

As I'm getting into my car I get a call from Frankie.

"Did you hear?"

Usually Frankie greets me by saying how much soccer sucks, but tonight he sounds different. Like something's wrong.

"What?"

"Seth. Did you hear what's going on?"

"No."

"Somebody tied him to a headstone in the cemetery right above the quarry."

I try to figure out what this even means. "What? I don't get it."

"I don't need to tell you who. It got out because of some people talking on Facebook."

"What got out?"

I have this sinking feeling in my gut.

"That they duct-taped Seth to a gravestone in a cemetery."

I shake my head and curse.

"Where are you?" I ask Frankie.

"Eating out with my folks. I'm leaving right now."

"So is Seth still there?"

"That's why I'm calling."

I curse again and start up the car. I know exactly where the cemetery is. It's not very far from where I am.

"It was Greg, right?" I curse a few more times.

"Calm down."

"I'm sick of this. Why are you calling me? Huh? Why not the police?"

I'm probably driving a little too fast. I'd love it if Greg's father the cop would try pulling me over.

"I knew something like this was going to happen," Frankie says. "Especially after the whole car incident."

"Why didn't Greg come after us?"

"He must have thought it was Seth. They made a spectacle of it. Like they made the guy into a Halloween attraction. Actually told people to come watch."

The houses fly by me as my windshield wipers get a work-out from the falling rain.

"And nobody took him down?"

"Not yet. That's why I'm coming. It's just—I'm not close. Half an hour away."

I take a wrong turn, have to go down another side street and turn around again.

"Have any idea where he is in the cemetery?"

"Look for a figure in a black ninja outfit taped to a headstone."

The way Frankie says it seems utterly crazy. "Is this a prank?"

"No. I wish it was."

I pull up to the cemetery and park. "I gotta go."

I slip my phone into my jeans and then zip up my jacket. It's cold enough to make the rain feel extra frigid. It's coming down hard now, and the wind is whipping it around.

This is wrong, all wrong.

Something tells me I shouldn't be here. That instead I should go to Marvel and stay with her.

But someone has to help Seth, so I walk around—then jog, then sprint—looking for him. Anger fuels me. I'm clenching my fists and my jaw and know I have to do something. This has to stop.

I reach a small road cutting through the cemetery and I stop, scanning the gravestones in every direction. Some tall, some tiny. Some flat on the ground. Some giant tombs big enough you can walk in them.

As with all the roads in my life at the moment, I'm desperate to know where this one leads. But I'm afraid, too. Something tells me I'm not going to like what I find. And it's going to be totally and completely out of my control.

54

The black figure stands like a statue at the front of the headstone, the duct tape used to strap him to the stone blending into his black ninja outfit. He's got a hooded mask as well, so I can't see his face. When I reach him and call out his name, I hear the sickest sort of stuffed-mouth grunt I will ever hear in my life. It sounds like someone being buried alive. I tell him it's going to be okay while I search for the tape, then realize that it's far too strong to simply rip off with my hands. He's attached to the gravestone by tape circling his neck and also his stomach. I cut my hands trying to undo it, then I use the sharpest key in my key ring. Oddly enough, it's the key to the record store.

"I'm trying, hold on," I say. "It's Brandon."

The rain is coming down hard. I keep hoping Frankie will arrive at any minute, but he doesn't. I keep trying to cut with the key. The tape finally starts ripping apart, and eventually I'm able to cut a line in the tape around his neck. I tear off the hood and see Seth's wet head looking like a sickly dog.

He's got more tape around his face, with a sock in his mouth. I pull it off and he chokes and starts to scream.

I've never heard such an awful sound in my life.

"You're okay," I say.

"They wanted to kill me," he says. "Look at this. They seriously were going to kill me. Get me off this thing. Get me off!"

He's moving and jerking around. I finally manage to get the rest of the tape off him. He helps peel himself off the stone and then he just crumples into the grass, crying. Cursing.

"I'm sorry, Seth. It's my fault. I did this."

"No. You. Didn't."

He's seething. He looks up at me with eyes that glare even in the darkness.

"It was Greg. He did this."

"I know. But my friends and I did that to his car."

"It doesn't matter. I told him I didn't do it, and he didn't listen. It doesn't matter. It's just going to get worse and worse and worse."

"Seth."

"I want to go home," he tells me.

"Yeah, okay."

Sometimes there's just nothing you can say, so you let the silence fill the space. I drive without speaking until Seth finally says something.

"Take me to Jeremy's place."

He's breathing heavily and is completely soaked.

"Don't you think you should—"

"Just take me there now."

"Are you sure you want to see Jeremy?"

He's the last person I'd add to this mix. Well, Jeremy or Uncle Crazy Carlos.

"I'm not going home looking like this," Seth says.

"Do you want to come over to—"

"Drive me over to Jeremy's now!"

His scream is animal-like. It's awful. I know he's freezing and is probably out of his mind with anger.

"What are you going to do?"

"Please, Brandon. Just do it."

"This is my fault," I tell him again.

"Yeah, I know what happened, whatever. It goes back a long ways. To what I did at the party to Sergio. Other things. They've been waiting."

"I'm going to deal with Greg," I tell him. "Tonight."

"I'm done with those guys. I'm done with all of it. School and everything."

"It's not going to happen again. The party—there's a party, and Greg's going to be there and I'll deal with him."

"Whatever," Seth says.

He's calming down as we drive toward Jeremy's house. Or at least his voice is starting to become lower.

"He's going to face consequences," I tell him. "This stuff has gone on too long."

"Whatever."

When I pull up to Jeremy's house, I notice that all the lights are off and there's not a trace of a person in sight.

"You think he's here?"

"Thanks for coming to get me. I owe you."

I stop him before he gets out. "Seriously, Seth. This all ends. Tonight. This wasn't right. This was criminal."

"I gotta go."

He gets out of my car and I watch his figure slowly seep into the dark night. It doesn't feel right, simply dropping him off at Jeremy's place. Nothing about Jeremy feels right, to be honest. But there's nothing I can do.

I can't add Seth to the *People I'm Trying to Protect* list. Marvel and Devon are enough. Plus my brothers.

I sigh because there's more I want to do but I can't. I haven't the foggiest idea how I'd even start.

55

If my steering wheel were Play-Doh, it'd be squeezed into oblivion by my grip. I called Frankie to say that I got Seth and I'm on my way to the party. I'm dealing with this. Now. Tonight. For a moment I think about going to the cops, but no. I'm going to the party first because I want to see that ugly, smug, stupid face. I want to smash it in.

The night feels different. Colder. Windier. Darker. I'm not sure. I felt it the moment I stepped out of Fascination Street. It's like a switch turns off. Of course, this is my imagination. It's just 'cause it's creepy, chilly old Halloween and it's *supposed* to feel that way, right? But I don't know. I swear I can feel something change.

Seeing a guy tied to a headstone in a cemetery might do that.

I get a text from Barton that says that he and Devon just arrived at the party.

Things getting crazy, he writes.

Heading there, I text him back. **Greg there?**

Rain douses the car as I drive. The sky continues to burst

bright with lightning. I think Halloweens are always cold around here. Cold and dark.

The silence makes me shiver. I miss Marvel already.

I shouldn't have left her. I should've stayed with her tonight.

At first I just assumed I was going to see my friends and have some fun and see some idiots in costumes. It's not about being seen, really. I just love laughing with the guys and staying away from home. That's all.

She should be coming with you.

Yeah, maybe. But I can't be with her every moment.
I figured I'd go to the party and then go back and see Marvel before the end of the night.

But now it's different. There's something I need to do.
I have to end this.

The street looks so long, so dark, the rain coming across sideways. Taryn's house is lit up like a glowing pumpkin. I park half a mile away, it seems, and walk toward the house with the pelting droplets soaking me. I look up at the sky and shiver, seeing the lightning. Those cutting bright lines in the night, showing everybody who's in control.

When I get to the front door, my face is wet and my hair messy and my clothes splattered. Great night to party. Or to fight.

Devon carries a plastic cup full of beer and I take it from him, then pound it. I've never done this in my life, but that's okay. I need a little help. Some liquid encouragement. I don't think of my father, don't think of anything, really. All I'm thinking about is Greg.

Loud. Music. People. Students. Laughing. Drinking. Costumes. Goofy. Silly. Stupid.

Images assault me as I stand in a living room packed with people. The guys are all talking at once.

"What'd he say?"

"What'd he do?"

"Where'd he go?"

I'm not answering their questions, however. I'm just looking around. Devon comes back carrying two cups of beer now, and I drain another.

"Whoa, what are you doing?" he asks.

"I don't care anymore," I say.

"I see." He looks a bit worried.

Frankie arrives and tries to calm me down. This has suddenly become a very big high school cliché. The party, the beer, the brawl. But I don't care.

"Where is he?"

"Brandon, I swear, don't," Frankie says. "Not tonight. Not after what they did."

I see Sergio walking around all drunk and smug and guilty. I know Greg has to be around somewhere.

I see Taryn in some tiny outfit. I think she's supposed to be Catwoman. I don't care.

I feel hands on my arms, and Frankie forces me to look at him.

"Do not do this, Brandon. Seriously."

I nod as if I'm agreeing.

Yeah right.

Then I see him standing in front of the fireplace. The fireplace with the mantel I remember so well. A mantel with all sorts of trophy pictures of the family. The golden family with all their pretty, wonderful smiles and light hair and glowing lives. There are other things too. A glass oval-shaped piece that's a trophy Taryn's mother won for some sort of thing—I don't know. Mementos from trips and events of their lives.

I look over at Devon, then smile.

"Uh-oh," he says.

"What?"

"I know that look."

"Yeah," I say, then add, "watch out. Things are about to get crazy."

I force my way through the crowd and approach Greg. He sees me walking toward him, his neck a round hunk of ham, his arrogant angry look making me hate him even more.

He laughs.

And that's when I start running toward him, slamming into him, blasting his back against the stone fireplace and clipping the side of his head against the mantel.

A guy could be killed like this, getting pummeled and bashing his head against a wooden beam.

But not Greg. Not meathead Greg.

I don't see what the others do around us. All I know is that Greg jumps up faster than I can imagine anybody jumping up, and then he uppercuts me with both of his hands. I literally feel lifted off the ground as I slam into several people behind me. Now I'm on the ground and Greg is over me. I hear yelling and screaming.

Greg leans over and punches my face. Again. And again. And the light and the darkness and the noise and the thunderstorms and the day and the night all sort of merge.

I am so stupid.

Didn't I see this in a dream? But no, the attacker was Carlos, and Seth was nearby.

Maybe I got the people wrong but the right situation?

The pain is blinding, and I see a crystal, startling light.

Marvel.

More commotion and screaming, and then I see a figure moving toward the one above me and then there's something happening.

It's Greg.

It's Frankie.

I see something in Greg's hand.

It's the award.

The winner of the mother of the year goes to Susan Ellsworth, mother of Taryn, and here's your trophy.

Now Greg's attacking Frankie and I try to help and do something but then the glass thing strikes my forehead.

Not a good year for my head.

Then good night.

56

"That's all I know. All I remember."

The two cops in my hospital room still want more. I'm not sure if they're going to arrest me or what.

"So you went there with the intent of assaulting Greg Packard?"

Mike Harden is the one sitting by my bed. He's a friendly guy, the one who I saw after the driving incident with my father. He was the one urging me to watch out for things.

"I didn't go to the party to do anything except see him. Tell him I found out what he did to Seth. Did you guys arrest him? What'd you do to him?"

"We're talking to all sides here, Brandon. The fact that Greg is Sergeant Packard's son makes it . . . complicated."

Mike looks back at the older cop with him. The guy's been quiet mostly and watching, adding only an occasional question.

"Greg is the one who did this to you, right?"

I nod. "Yeah. I mean, I pushed him, and then he began to punch me in the face."

"He cracked your skull with a glass trophy," Harden says. "Then broke his own quarterback's arm."

I look at both of them. "What?"

"Yeah. Franklin Davis. His throwing arm is fractured. He was trying to get Greg off of you, and the guy went off. Quite the scene. A dozen cops and an ambulance for you two. Really messy."

I feel like throwing up.

"I don't know what to say."

"You haven't heard from anybody who was at the party since, right?"

"No. I've been—I've been here."

It's nine in the morning.

I've been here this long?

"Are you going to arrest me?"

I see Harden give the other cop a knowing look. A bad one, one that makes me think I really don't want to hear what it's all about.

"What's going on?"

"Have you heard anything—any word—from Devon Teed?"

I look at them. I've already checked my phone. Nothing. No text, no call. Nothing.

"No."

"He's missing, according to his parents and everybody else. Hasn't been heard from since the party ended abruptly."

"Have you checked—did you ask Frankie? And what about Barton?"

"You're the last one we're asking. Had to wait until you gained consciousness."

"Was it Greg—did he have anything to do with it?"

Harden only shakes his head. "Greg spent the night in jail, so no. He didn't have anything to do with Devon's disappearance. Considering the last six months around here, lots of folks are worried. Really worried."

Something about the way he says "really worried" makes *me* do the same.

The cops stay another ten minutes, asking me questions and seeing if there's any more information I can give them. Then they leave. Before they do, Harden gives me a sympathetic look. His partner has left the room.

"I know you were just helping out a kid who was being bullied. I commend you for that. Especially considering how big Greg is compared to you."

I feel more woozy than ever.

"Do you think something happened to Devon?"

"I don't know. I hope not."

But his grim face says it all.

When they leave I look up at the ceiling and then suddenly and uncontrollably start to cry.

57

I text about twenty people to see if they've heard from Devon.
Then I spend half an hour answering people who ask how
I'm doing. But nobody knows anything about Devon. He
disappeared after the party. Barton couldn't find him after
the insanity of the cops coming and Frankie and me being
carted off in ambulances, so he went home with other friends.
Devon didn't respond to texts after the party.

It's like he got into his Jeep and then just *disappeared*.

Nobody knows. Everybody worries. And I feel absolutely
nauseous.

*Because you're scared. For maybe the first time since Artie was
found dead, you're really, really terrified.*

I text and call Marvel, but she doesn't answer. Instead, she
appears at my door.

The face looking in at me isn't a happy one, however.

"Hi, Berry," I say, trying to make a joke.

She comes to the edge of my bed and gently touches the
side of my head, the side that throbs in pain, the one that's all

bandaged up. She opens her mouth to say something, then starts to weep.

"Hey now," I say. "Come on. It's okay. Seriously."

Marvel holds her face in her hands until I manage to pry one away and hold it.

"I'm fine."

"This is all my fault," she says.

"Yeah. I'm glad you sent me to that party and made me get into a fight with Greg. Thanks a lot."

"No. Not that but this. All of this. I just . . . maybe Taryn is right. About all the bad things that have happened since I've come here—"

"Stop it. Stop."

"It's true."

"No. What's true is that Taryn's the next one I'm getting in a fight with."

Her big, dark, round eyes look at me with such a deep, sad look. It's more painful than the feeling I have in my brain.

"I knew and yet I just—I ignored it," Marvel says with a weary tone.

"You knew what? What are you talking about?"

"I knew the truth. I knew what I was *supposed* to do, but I didn't listen."

"Please, Marvel, don't. Please don't."

"Don't what?" She shakes her head and looks like she's staring at a dead person.

"Don't make this into *that* issue. The whole God thing."

"But it is. Don't you see? Don't you—I know you think— Well, I'm not sure I know what you really think. But I know that you don't believe. That's it's not real and personal to you, but it's real and personal to me. I know what I've seen and what I've heard. And I heard very specifically that I couldn't and shouldn't, and yet . . . yet I wanted it. I was selfish. I wanted it for me."

"You wanted what?" I ask.

"You. I wanted *you*, you dummy. I wanted to see you smile and I wanted you in my arms and I wanted to smell you on me and I wanted as much as I could have. I shouldn't have. And I won't. Not anymore. Because bad things continue to happen."

"I made a mistake," I say. "I got angry—I lost it. I just— you should've seen him hanging there, Marvel. It was awful. I mean—I'm never going to forget that. For someone to do that. It's grotesque. Seriously."

"I know. But you almost got killed."

"No, I didn't."

"You were unconscious. Frankie told me everything."

"Have you seen him?"

"Yeah."

"How is he? Where is he?"

"He got out early this morning. He's doing fine."

"That guy broke his arm."

She nods, wiping more tears.

"Devon . . ."

I shake my head, wanting to encourage her. "He probably just freaked out that two of his best friends got mauled. He's probably in Nebraska driving around."

She breathes in and closes her eyes. "I was supposed to be 'helping.' I'm supposed to be here to help and all I keep seeing is people I love and care for hurting."

I don't know what to say. I honestly don't.

"Maybe you can ask the Big Guy for some answers."

"Don't be like that."

"I'm just saying," I tell her. "I have no answers and haven't heard anything."

"Have you asked?"

"No."

"Then maybe you should," Marvel says. "Maybe that's the very first thing you need to do."

"You're trying to save me, aren't you?"

"If I could I would, Brandon. But I can't. I'm not the one to do that."

"It's going to be okay."

But I don't believe it, and that's clear in my voice.

Devon and Frankie and Greg and Seth and now Marvel.

How are things ever going to be *okay*? It's a cruel joke.

"I have to do the right thing, Brandon."

"And what's that?"

"I need to let you be. I need to stop—stop this. Stop us. Stop this thing."

"You can't."

"No, I have to," she says. "Now. This moment. I can't play around anymore. There are lives at stake. There's something—something is happening and I don't know what, but I'm afraid it's going to just keep getting worse."

"Marvel," I say, trying to reach out, but I can't touch her. She's too far away.

"I'm sorry, Brandon."

"You can't. Seriously. Not now. I mean—look at me."

"I know."

"I got hit by a truck and now you're driving a train into me."

For a second she laughs between more tears. "That was funny."

"I try."

"I'm here—I'm alive—because of God's will. He chose me for a reason. Because of this thing I'm going to do. And I'm afraid I've become distracted. And the enemy has managed to come in and set up fort."

"Are you saying I'm the enemy?"

She shakes her head. "No. My flawed heart is the enemy. My selfishness and my vanity. I want what I want. And I wanted you. So I took you."

"Take me again."

"No."

"I'm free of charge. I'm a deal. Come on."

"Stop," Marvel says. "And stop smiling like that."

"You can't break up with me now. No way."

"I have to."

"I'll win you back."

"No."

"You can't resist my charms. I will come knocking on your door at midnight bringing graham crackers and cranberry juice."

"Stop. Please."

"I will take you to hidden gardens where people dance and where homemade salsa is made."

She's crying more.

"I'm trying to make you smile, but man, I don't think it's working."

"Please don't make this any harder than it already is," she says.

"Oh, the worst line ever," I tell her. "I'm going to make it hard all right. I'm going to make it impossible."

She sits down in the same chair Officer Harden was sitting in.

"Oh, so you're not going to leave?"

"I can still be here for you," Marvel says. "I'm still your friend. You need a friend, right?"

"Yes. And a maid and a study companion and someone to shack up with at night."

She shakes her head. "The IV has surely gotten to your head."

"Yes."

I can still see the look on her face and I want her to have hope.

"Devon's going to be okay," I say. "Seriously. It's just—I'm sure he just—I'm sure it's something."

Yeah. I'm sure it's something. Good or bad. It's something.

58

Mom heads out the sliding glass doors toward the hospital parking lot. This is the second time this year—second time in just a few months—that she's picking me up from the hospital. She didn't say much to me except for telling me how lucky I am and that she's glad the guy who did it got arrested. She doesn't cry in front of me but she has swollen eyes, so I figure she's already done her share. We talk a little about Devon but it's all too much for her, so I just try to encourage her the same way I did Marvel, saying Devon's going to show up again.

But I'm not so sure. I keep texting him. Keep calling. And nothing comes back. The calls just go into voicemail.

As I'm waiting in a wheelchair (something they forced me to use while I'm leaving the hospital because of my head injury) for Mom to pull the car up, I look around the waiting room. That's when I see him.

Slicked back dark hair, chiseled features, cold black eyes. Just sitting watching me.

It's Carlos, wearing a leather coat and sitting in a corner chair just staring at me. He's not reading anything, doesn't seem to be waiting for anybody. Marvel's already gone, so I know he's not waiting for her.

Soon Mom is back, and I step off the wheelchair. Carlos keeps watching me, his eyes unmoving.

If he's here to send a message, then message heard.

Loud and clear.

My brothers cheer me up, and thankfully Dad is nowhere to be found. It looks like both my season and Frankie's season are over. I'm eager to talk with him, but I can't leave the house yet. Mom tells me I won't be leaving it for a long time. She says I'm grounded, and that was *before* hearing the news about Devon.

I look at the walls surrounding me and wonder if I'm going to be seeing this house a lot more. I sure hope not. I'll lose whatever's left of my mind.

A text comes in and I look quickly, hoping to see that it's from either Devon or Marvel. But it's Frankie.

You okay?

I'm so sorry man, I reply. **I'm fine.**

You didn't look fine to me.

I'm glad they arrested him.

He's been out all day, Frankie writes.

So what happens now?

I don't know. I don't want to know.

I want that guy to pay.

Obviously.

I'm sorry you got involved, I text him.

I was the one who got involved. You didn't force me to come over there.

You might've saved my life. That's what one of the nurses told me.

Go ahead.

I look at the text. **What?**

Just go ahead and say it.

What?

"Frankie Davis. You're my hero."

Even now he can joke. Which is a good thing.

Frankie Davis. You definitely are my hero.

Great, he responds.

Any news on Devon?

No.

You don't think . . .

I can't even write it out.

No.

Yeah, me neither, I write.

There's no way. Not Devon.

I know. Oh—by the way. I'm grounded. For life maybe.

Yeah, I'm in trouble too. I bet you anything Greg isn't.

Course not.

You're right, you know? He totally let me get sacked in that last game.

I know.

My season was already over.

I want to ask him about college scholarships and acceptance and all that, but I can't. I can't take any more sadness today.

I'll see you soon, I text. **I'm sorry buddy.**

It's all good. Let me know if you hear from Devon.

You too.

That night, before going to sleep, I text Devon one more time.

Man are you there? You got everybody really freaked out. If you can read this—the joke's over. People are thinking we have another Artie Duncan happening. That's definitely NOT COOL. Let me know you're okay. Okay?

I expect to hear nothing. But then I look at my phone and see the dots showing that someone's texting back.

See he's okay! I knew it. I knew Devon was okay.

Devon is dead and if you stay so curious, your pretty little girlfriend will be next.

The text almost burns in my hand. I want to throw my phone, but realize this could be Devon. So I text back. Again. And again. Asking if it's him. Telling him to stop. Cursing at him. Trying to get any other reply. But none comes. None except this initial threatening, devastating sentence.

I refuse to believe it. Refuse.

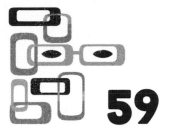

59

In the middle of the night I get up and feel wobbly as my pulse throbs in my head.

I can hear Marvel's words as I move.

I think about her uncle in the hospital.

Was that a threat? A warning? A message? A sign?

I crawl back into bed and breathe in and out. I'm scared. Really scared.

God, can you help me a little? I need some help. Seriously. Starting with Devon. Don't let him be dead. Please, God, don't let him be dead.

I don't want to sleep because I don't want to see what nightmare awaits.

60

Okay, Marvel. I've texted you almost as much as I've texted Devon, and I've gotten nothing. So now I'm e-mailing. I know what you might be feeling, and it's okay. It's okay to be afraid. I'm afraid too. But that doesn't mean you need to avoid me or stay away. You don't have to.

Marvel—we need each other.

I don't know what's happening, and all I can say is that this is NOT God blaming you or cursing you for something you did. Love will never be a bad thing. Never. I know you love me 'cause you told me. And you know I love you. That's not going away suddenly like blowing out a birthday candle.

So show me. Please, Marvel. Come to my house this evening. Please. You don't have to say anything. Just come and stand by my side. I want to hold you and know you're there. It'll be fine. Nobody will bother us. I promise.

Whatever is happening—we'll figure it out together. Okay?

Please, Marvel.

I'll see you later.
Brandon

I'm sitting in the same place I usually sit on the couch. It's ten o'clock and I'm still holding out hope. Even though I haven't heard anything from Marvel—not a reply to my e-mail and not a text or a call—I still believe she might stop by. I continue to listen for the knock on the door. I keep waiting and checking my phone and waiting more.

I wait another hour, then decide to text her again. But deep down inside, I know. Everything is different.

Devon's going to show up.

I have to believe this.

Carlos is just bullying me like all of the other bullies in my life.

I have to trust this.

Marvel still cares for me and she'll come back to me. Maybe not tonight but then tomorrow or the next day.

I have to know this.

But I'm waiting for her and every single thing I have inside in my heart is out there for her to know and to see. I'm absolutely an open book.

And I'm waiting.

But Marvel never shows up. She never calls or texts.

And there's no music playing in the background and nobody holding my hand and the lights inside this room feel like they're changing from a warm orange to a lifeless pale white.

Soon enough, I turn off the television and the lights and then look at this space of darkness. I don't feel like it's my home anymore.

I head up the stairs and enter my room. Tonight, for some reason, I lock the door.

I keep picturing Devon in my mind. Seth on that grave-stone. Greg and his ugly, smug smile. Frankie with a broken arm. My father waiting. Carlos at the hospital, watching.

I can't do anything. Except, maybe, of course, the obvious.

"God, are you there? Are you? Are you really there like Marvel makes it sound? 'Cause I don't know what's happen-ing. I have no idea where I'm going to go or what I'm going to find."

I feel weird talking like this, because I don't think anybody is listening. But I want to believe someone is there listening. Watching. Knowing. Loving.

"God. I just—let Devon be okay. Let Devon be fine."

I feel weird and I also feel scared. These words . . . they don't bring comfort. They only bring confusion.

I really, really want to believe. I want to grab those stars and smuggle them away to some better place. And I want to take Marvel with me. Then never, ever come back.

But I'm afraid Marvel—and Devon—are both long gone.

ACKNOWLEDGMENTS

Thanks . . .

To Sharon, Kylie, Mackenzie, and Brianna for letting me be the most emotional person in this house.

To my parents and in-laws for letting me borrow money.

To my extended family. I will let you borrow the girls if I can borrow some money.

To Meg Wallin, for green-lighting this series. It wouldn't exist without you. Thanks.

To L. B. Norton, for getting rid of the dead horse. I still would have put it in myself, but nope. No dead horse. Readers will never see the dead horse.

To Claudia Cross, for not telling me out loud that I'm insane.

To NavPress, for partnering with Tyndale. Because it takes two awesome publishers to publish an awesome author like me.

To Don Pape, for not only green-lighting my first teen series, but realizing you need to continue to publish me, thus coming over to NavPress to work. What a fan. What a man. Lending a helping hand. Such a Canadian.

To Jimmy Wayne, and Mark Schultz, and Thompson Square, and the *Home Run* film family, and the Celebrate Recovery family, and Mac and Mary Owen, and Dorothy Shackleford and Blake Shelton, and the Harding family, and *The Remaining* movie family, and those bearded men from West Monroe and their families: all of you are awesome for inviting me into your worlds for a brief literary adventure.

And last but not least, to Chris Buckley, who is starting his sophomore year and starting to lose his way just a bit. Oh dear. Hang on, buddy.

PLAYLISTS

MARVEL'S IPOD

1. "17 Hours" by Emma Louise
2. "Pieces" by Andrew Belle
3. "Atlas" by Coldplay
4. "Holding On for Life" by Broken Bells
5. "Rooftops" by Kye Kye
6. "Help Me Lose My Mind" by Disclosure
7. "Duele" by Carla Morrison
8. "XO" by Beyoncé
9. "Shyer" by London Grammar
10. "Sun" by Sleeping at Last
11. "There Is a Place" by Morten Harket
12. "All the Days" by HAERTS

HARRY'S CD

1. "Crystal" by Stevie Nicks
2. "One More Time" by The Cure
3. "El Cóndor Pasa (If I Could)" by Simon & Garfunkel
4. "Ask" by The Smiths
5. "Singalong Junk" by Paul McCartney
6. "Crests of Waves" by Coldplay
7. "Spirits (Having Flown)" by the Bee Gees
8. "Be Kind to My Mistakes" by Kate Bush
9. "Sara" by Fleetwood Mac
10. "Together in Electric Dreams" by Human League
11. "Blue Dress" by Depeche Mode
12. "More than This" by Roxy Music